THE ALIEN'S GLIMPSE

GRACE KENSINGTON

1

———

Rain felt her hands trembling as they drew closer to the shape of the planet in the distance. It had been so long since the first time that they had traveled from the desolate planet of Penthos to Uoria, but the feeling was far different this time. When the Nyx 23 mission was first overtaken, their ship sabotaged so that they had no control over its navigation or communication, they were traveling from one unknown planet to another. The existence of the planet that would come to be known as Penthos had been only just identified and they knew nothing about it. The planet that she now knew as Uoria hadn't even been identified. The very concept that it existed wasn't debated, there was simply no knowledge that the planet even existed.

In the moments that they were falling toward Uoria during their first journey, Rain hadn't had the opportunity to watch as the ground came closer and closer beneath the ship. Instead she had been frantically trying to get to the control room, wanting to try to fulfill her responsibility to reclaim control of the ship. It was Etan, though, that had taken her focus away from the controls. She knew now that there was nothing that she could have done, even if she had stepped over Etan and grasped the controls. The ship had been taken out of their power and no matter what she had done or tried to do, there would have been no way that she would have been able to reclaim the ability to pilot the ship. The weapons that the Valdicians had used to disable the StarCity were impenetrable and any efforts that she had tried to put forth to override what they had done would have been completely futile.

Just as much as there was nothing that she could have done about the sabotage of the Valdicians, there was nothing that she could have done to help Etan. He was beyond anyone's help by the time that she had found him, destroying himself before he had to watch as the rest of the crew that he was supposed to lead, guide, and protect suffered the catastrophic crash. In those moments, it had felt nearly hopeless. Rain had never been one to allow herself to completely give up any hope that she might have, no matter what the situation. She had always been determined and almost aggressive in her pursuit of what she wanted. As a child, she had been told that she wouldn't be able to fulfill the dream that she had for herself to be a part of the elite research and paramilitary department that she dreamed of joining. She had been told that she wouldn't be able to handle the education or the training that it would require just to earn a place in the program, much less be a part of any of the missions. There were times when it was only her hope, her dedication to herself, that kept her going. Too many times she had felt alone and like she had no one who cared if she managed to accomplish anything that she had set her mind to doing. In those times, she could only rely on her own mind to push her through.

It had been hard to hold to that hope when they were hurtling toward the unknown, seemingly empty planet below. She didn't know if they were even going to survive the crash. What they might find if they did barely even crossed her mind. She could only hope for her next breath, one right after the other, hoping that she would be able to take in another breath, hoping that when the ship finally did crash that she would either survive it or die quickly, hoping that if she did survive she would know what she should do next. Though it had been a struggle, it had been her hope, the same determination that she had always had, that had brought her from breath to breath and kept her going as they went through the rest of the fall, crashed into the planet, and began the new life that waited ahead of them on their new planet.

Now the hope inside Rain was stronger and she felt more confident as they approached Uoria. The power of the ship beneath her hands almost felt like a vindication, redemption for that horrific day. She could control the descent of the ship now. She knew what waited below them and what she would do when they finally rested on the ground again. It restored her faith in herself and invigorated her against the battle that they had left and the war that lay ahead.

When the surface of Uoria was close enough, she set the signal for those aboard to secure themselves in their passenger pods. She knew that not everyone would be able to follow that instruction. Those still in the infirmary would have to simply lock their beds into place, secure belts across their bodies, and hope that they remained in place. Rain took one hand away from the controls to secure her own hardness so that it held her tightly to the pilot chair. As the belts clicked into place, cuffs emerged from the base of the chair and locked around her legs. Another secured around her chest. The pressure was reassuring in that she knew they would protect her as they landed. At the same time it was frightening, reminding her that she couldn't move, that she was stuck in place until the ship was fully landed and the built-in restraint system released. The thought that she was completely unable to move, to get away from the chair even if she wanted to, made anxiety rise in her stomach and squeeze in her chest. If something was to happen and the sabotage by the Valdicians came back into effect, there would be no way for her to save herself or anyone else in the ship.

Rain took a breath and tightened her grip on the controls. She didn't know if everyone had made it into the passenger pods, but she couldn't wait any longer. They were too close to the surface of Uoria to continue moving forward. She needed to start the descent. She felt the slight sinking feeling as the ship started to move down. It would only be a matter of seconds, but it felt like an eternity as she willed the massive machine to bring itself down. She hoped that she was close to where she had intended them to come down. Though it would have seemed appropriate for them to land in close to the same spot as the original crash, this would have been too far from the Mikana kingdom or the human settlement. Instead, she had planned for them to come down in between the two, close enough that they would be able to get to the kingdom quickly and be only a brief trip to the human settlement as long as the Denynso had done as they asked and brought the small vehicles Athan had revealed to them back to the kingdom from the orchard in the compound.

She wished that Lynx was with her. She would be more comfortable with him beside her, reassuring her with just his presence. But she took comfort in knowing that at least this time everyone in their pods would be protected. Many of the deaths that occurred when the StarCity crashed were among those who were working in the ship, moving around the various rooms and systems rather than securing themselves before landing. Of course, the pods had been different then. They were nowhere near as strong and effective as the ones in the ships now. Rain's mind was still filled with horrifying images of exploring the far-flung wreckage and finding bodies tangled in the remnants of destroyed pods, some killed by the shattered shells of the very pods that were meant to protect them.

The planet was coming closer. It was just ahead. She braced herself and continued to guide the ship down. There was no landing platform to support the ship, meaning that they would have to land straight onto the ground, which would be a far less comfortable landing. Finally, the bottom of the ship touched down and Rain felt the rumble of the impact go through her. She held her breath, waiting for the ship to settle and tell her that the journey was over. Seconds later the ship fell still and the breath streamed from her lungs. The restraints released, enabling her to remove the harness that she had locked into place and stand from the chair. She had done it. They were back on Uoria.

2
———

Creia paced back and forth across the entrance gate to the Mikana kingdom. He felt like he had been walking there for hours, but he couldn't bring himself to stop. Mina had received communication from Nylek informing her that they were on their way from Penthos, and while it was a relief and a comfort to know that they were coming, she had said that his voice was weak. The Denynso king knew that this meant that the warrior was injured, and he was worried about what they had endured already.

"They will be here when they get here," Theia said as she approached, holding out a cup toward Creia. "You are going to exhaust yourself. Remember, you are not fully recovered yet."

"I want to be here when they arrive," Creia said. "I need to see them." He took the cup from his mate and took a long sip of the sweet nectar. "Thank you," he said, leaning down to give Theia a kiss.

She swept the sides of her robes around her, shuddering

against some chill that Creia didn't feel. Seeing her reaction, though, brought his attention even harder to the horizon. The empathetic skills of his mate were unparalleled. Though she didn't have the same abilities as Loralia, allowing her to know what they were feeling and experiencing their emotions as if they were her own, Theia was able to sense the energy of those around her, especially when they were at their extremes. The chill that she was feeling now was likely the pain and intensity that the group was feeling now as they approached. Finally, he saw dark figures in the distance. They moved as an amorphous unit, sometimes appearing to be one and other moments separating so that Creia was able to identify the individual figures.

The numbers that he saw didn't make sense. There weren't enough of them. There should have been far more with them. Creia felt the wind whipping across his face before he realized that he was running. There should have been pain as his feet hit the ground and his body pushed harder than it had since before his imprisonment, but there was nothing. The intensity of the worry that coursed through him was enough to mask anything that he might experience. He might suffer later, but for now he had to get to them. He needed to know what was happening.

As he approached he saw that the group was working together to carry two of the men. One was Nylek, the other Kyven. He scanned the faces of the others in the group, but didn't see Maxim, Oro, Jonah, or many of the others that he expected would be with them.

"Creia!" Ivy shouted as they drew closer.

"Ivy," Creia said, reaching for the human woman. "What's happening? Where is everyone?"

Ivy shook her head. She appeared drawn and breathless,

and Creia was immediately even more worried about Maxim and the others.

"We are the only ones who are here," she told him. "The others are still on Penthos, and on Earth."

"On Earth?" Creia asked, horrified by the revelation. "They didn't make it to you?"

Ivy shook her head again.

"No," she said. "Oro, Jonah, Azrael, and Ariella used the vehicle that Jonah and Rain designed to get to Earth to assist the ones that Ryan had captive there, but they haven't returned. Maxim, Zyyr, and the others are still on Penthos. They have been able to keep the hybrid army back, but the conflict will only get worse. They need all the help that they can get. They need the army and weapons from here."

"We need to get these men to the clinic," Rain said, gesturing to the two men being carried. "Is Rey in the kingdom?"

"Yes," Creia said, "he's there, so are the doctors. What has happened to these men?"

"Nylek was attacked by a group of hybrids. Kyven was injured by a creature who lives under the ground on Penthos. We've done everything that we can to treat them, but they are still weak. They need more food, water, and treatment. We brought them back here so that they would be in less danger. This is Elon," Rain said, gesturing to the unfamiliar man in the group. "He is a human medic. He was on the shuttle when we were traveling toward Earth. He's been helping take care of the men."

Creia could hear tension in Rain's voice, but he didn't question her. For now, they needed to get the men to the Mikana clinic. He reached forward and swept Nylek into his arms, freeing the smaller man from the burden of trying to support the massive warrior. They started back toward the kingdom as fast as they could and as they approached, Creia called out to Theia.

"Get the doctors," he called. "Tell them to get to the clinic. These men need help."

They rushed through the gate and into the kingdom, heading directly toward the clinic that rested in the center. He carefully lowered Nylek to one of the beds and turned to watch them help Kyven into place. Out of the corner of his eye he saw Athan back out of the clinic and start running toward the homes at the back of the kingdom. The Denynso king backed away as the doctors came into the room and headed for the two wounded men, then turned to Ivy.

"How is Maxim?" he asked.

Ivy nodded.

"He's well," she said. "He's gotten through the battles without serious injury."

"That's good to hear. I am surprised to see you here instead of with him there."

Ivy looked down, her eyes brimming with tears.

"He sent me here," she said. "He wants to keep me safe."

He knew that there was more to it than just that Maxim didn't want her on the dangerous planet. She had already been engaged in battle with them. He knew that she was capable of taking care of herself, or could at the very least remain out of the way. Maxim needed her like the Denynso needed their mates, and Creia couldn't imagine him sending her away without a good reason. Before he could ask anything else, she looked back up at him, her eyes suddenly clear and stern.

"Did you gather all of the supplies that he asked you to?" she asked.

Creia nodded.

"Most of them," he said. "We brought the vehicles from

the orchard and have some supplies from the Denynso compound. Ellora hasn't given us permission yet to go into the war room to get the weapons that Maxim described. She doesn't want to even talk to us. It's like she's trying to ignore that the war is even happening."

"She can't do that," Ivy said. "Maxim needs those weapons. We aren't going to be able to get through this with just the supplies that they have. Even when the others arrive from Earth, there aren't going to be enough weapons or rations to support them. She can't just not allow them to get what we need."

"I can do as I please."

Creia saw Ivy whip around to face Ellora where she stood at the door to the clinic. The woman looked angry and drawn, but there was a sadness in her eyes that was impossible to ignore.

"Ellora," Ivy said, taking a step toward her.

"Where is my son?" she asked.

Creia stepped out of the way so that she could see Kyven lying on the bed further into the clinic. She immediately pushed past him, rushing to the side of the bed and leaning over her son. She took his head and reached forward to touch the side of his face.

"Kyven," she said softly. "It's Mama. I'm here."

Kyven's eyes opened and smiled at his mother.

"I'm alright," he said. "I'm healing. It wasn't serious."

"It *was* serious," Emerie said from the other side of the bed. "The Meldor nearly killed you, and we don't know what kind of toxins it had on its claws. That's why Maxim sent you back here."

"I should be there with him," he said. "I should be fighting alongside him, not lying in this bed."

"You can't be there with him," Emerie said. "You aren't in

any condition to be fighting. You need to recover, and when you do, you can be of good use to him."

"Listen to her, son," Ellora said sternly. "She's right. You might want to be with your brother and I'm sure that he wants you to be with him, but if you are injured, there's no way that you are going to be able to give him the support that he needs. You will be in more danger and you will put the rest of them in danger as well. If you stay here and focus on recuperating, you will be strong enough to fight, though I wish that you wouldn't."

"Why?" Kyven asked, shifting as if trying to sit up. "Why shouldn't I fight?" Emerie touched her hand to his shoulder and laid her mate back down onto the bed, but Kyven kept staring at his mother intently. "It's like you don't want us to win," he said. "You don't care what's happening to all of us."

"I do care, Kyven," Ellora said, "but I have already lived so much of my life suffering the loss of my husband. I don't want to lose you and your brother as well. All of this has happened before. There has been struggling and fighting for your entire life, and there will continue to be in all parts of the galaxy, in all parts of the universe throughout the rest of time. You don't have to be a part of it."

"There will be fighting," Creia said, stepping forward, "but it won't be like this. There is so much more happening than has ever happened before. There is so much more than any of us have ever known. This isn't a grudge, Ellora. This isn't something that we are fighting just for the sake of fighting."

"How do you know that?" she asked. "You just came here. I have never seen you before now. How am I to know that I can trust what you have to say about this war? We were peaceful until your kind showed up here. We hadn't seen war since the battle when Aegeus died. Then your warriors came here and suddenly everything has fallen apart around us."

"Don't talk to him that way," Kyven said. "This is not Creia's fault. He didn't cause this. If it hadn't been for the Denynso, we never would have learned what we have. We wouldn't have found out the extent of what's happening, and things would be much worse very soon. Besides, Papa..."

Athan stepped up to the side of the bed with a sound that silenced Kyven.

"You should rest now," he said. "The doctors will take care of you and Emerie will bring you something to eat soon. Ellora, you should go back home for now. They need good food and drinks to restore their strength."

Creia saw Ellora look down at her son with questions in her eyes. It was obvious that she knew he had more to say and he waited for her to ask, but she didn't. She straightened slowly, releasing Kyven's hand as she went, and then looked at Athan and nodded.

"Alright," she said. She lifted her eyes to Emerie. "Come to my house later and get food for these men."

"I will," Emerie said.

Creia watched as Athan carefully place a hand in the of Ellora's back and guided her away from the clinic. He turned back to Kyven and looked down at him.

"What were you going to say about your father?" he asked.

"He's still alive," Kyven said. "He didn't die in that battle."

"Are you sure?" Creia asked.

Kyven nodded.

"Ryan told us himself. At least until then, he was still alive."

"He's been holding him all these years?" the king asked.

"Yes," Kyven said. "They captured him during that battle and he has had him since. I can't imagine what he's been doing to him."

"I can," Creia said, his mind immediately flashing back to the horrific time that he had spent captive by the Valdicians, his very thoughts controlled by Ryan as he was forced to stare into the screen attached to his head for hours at a time. Starved and tortured, he had barely lived, and he had been held only a brief time. "Did he say that he would keep him alive?" he asked.

Kyven shook his head.

"No," he said. "He wants me and Maxim, though. Maybe if we're able to keep fighting and can resist him, that will keep him alive."

"If he wants you and Maxim, Aegeus isn't safe. He knows where you are and that he can get to you. That's enough to make it no longer necessary for him to keep your father around. If he decides that Aegeus has become too much trouble, or that he doesn't need him anymore, or even just that he wants to be as vindictive as possible, he will kill your father without a second thought. We need to get to him as quickly as we can if we want to keep him alive."

"The group needs rest for tonight," Kyven said. "We can't simply go back."

"I know," Creia said. "There is still preparation to be done, but now that you are all here, you can help. We'll do everything that we can to gather what we'll need, and then we'll go back. We can only hope that Maxim will be able to hold them off on his own until we get back, or that the rest of the group will make it to Penthos in time to help him. This has to end."

He started toward the door to the clinic and heard Kyven call after him.

"Where are you going?" he asked.

"I need to go talk to Ellora," he said. "Maxim gave instructions for what we needed to do to get ready for this war. I remember fighting alongside your father when we were young. I know the importance of the weapons that he collected. He wouldn't have done that if he didn't know that something was going to happen, if he didn't have a plan already in motion. She needs to let us access to war room."

"No," Kyven said. "Don't."

"Why not?" Creia asked. "We don't have time to wait for her to decide that she is going to accept what's happening. We can't give the power of the future of the galaxy to her and her denials."

"I know," Kyven said, "but she won't listen to you. Let Athan talk to her. She doesn't trust anyone like she trusts Athan. Give him time. Do whatever else you can to get everyone ready, but let him talk to her."

"Alright," Creia said, "but I can't just give them endless time. We have to prepare. We have to get to them."

He turned and left the clinic, walking out into the growing evening with too much energy and anticipation to even think about sleeping. There had to be something else that he could do. Until they were on the ship heading back to Penthos, he wouldn't be able to allow himself to stop or to rest.

3

Jonah stepped into the infirmary as quietly as he could. He didn't want to disturb anyone who was sleeping inside. Though they had made the decision to stay on their own, he felt strangely responsible for the wounded hybrids and pregnant women who remained in the infirmary. Before Pyra left he had helped the women move into the original infirmary, joining them all together so that they could be safe and secure together. It made Jonah feel more comfortable knowing that they were in the same space, protected simply by merit of being closer to one another. Being out of sight of others was when they were in the most danger, and it was important to him that he do everything that he could to help keep them as safe as he could while he was alone with them on Earth. He didn't know what he would be able to do for them if further danger did arise, but for then he could at least offer his presence.

Everyone inside seemed to be resting comfortably and he stepped out, closing the door as gently behind him as he could. He went back into the chamber where he had slept since they first arrived in the abandoned medical building and settled onto his bed. The others had been gone for only a few hours, and the reality of the situation was beginning to settle in for Jonah. He had been completely confident about the decision that he was making when he told Pyra that he was going to stay behind to look further into the medical files while the others went to Penthos, but now it was truly sinking in that the rest of those from Uoria had gotten onto that shuttle, leaving him behind to handle whatever might happen on his own. Though he knew that they were doing what they needed to do just as he was doing what he needed to do, it was also unnerving to know that he couldn't just turn to them if something else happened.

Jonah's hand settled onto the stack of medical files beside his bed and he felt a slight shock of energy move through his palm, reminding him of why he had decided to stay, of how pressing it was for him to remain behind so that he could try to understand what could have happened so many years before that could have had an impact that was still lingering now. He didn't understand what it could possibly be that would make the doctor not just leave his file behind, but to close the door to the examination room and apparently walk away, leaving that space untouched and unchanged even as the rest of the medical building continued to operate and was then closed down. Why didn't anyone open the door? Why didn't anyone question why the doctor never used the examination room again? Why didn't they look at it or take the things out of it when they were closing the medical building down in preparation to build the new section of the hospital.

A thought suddenly occurred to him and Jonah sat up straighter. The new building. Why would they build the new building around the old medical facility? Eden and the other human women had told him that they had planned to replace the old University for several years before they actually got started on the construction. All the other buildings were completely leveled so that they could build the new facilities in their places. They even built a new research hospital on the other side of the campus, establishing a much larger and more advanced facility for medical research and treatment for people who studied at the University as well as the other programs that used the campus as their headquarters, such as the department that bore Nyx 23. It didn't make sense that of all the buildings that they would keep, they would choose to preserve an old, outdated hospital ward that they would seal completely within the laboratory so that it wasn't just inaccessible, but fully forgotten until now.

The thought brought a strange feeling to Jonah's stomach. He knew that this was so much more than they could have imagined. The further that they thought that they went, the closer that they thought they were getting to finally laying the conflict to rest, the more and more it seemed to unravel, revealing further and further layers. He thought of those who had left the basement on their way to the transportation bay so that they could get to Penthos. He hoped that they had made it and were on their way, but he knew deep in his chest that there was a possibility that they hadn't survived the short but treacherous journey from the laboratory building to the vehicles that would take them off of Earth and back to the nearly barren planet. There was also a possibility that they had gotten part of the way there and then encountered the Valdicians or more of the hybrids and were captured, taken prisoner and forced into another area of Ryan's compound of torture. This, Jonah thought, was likely a far worse possibility than even a brutal and bloody death in battle.

Jonah looked down at his hand on the files again. He needed to understand what happened, not just for him but for every person whose name appeared in these files. Their lives had all been taken, stolen from them, by something. Even those of them who had survived no longer had the lives that they thought that they were going to, and no longer had the potential to do what they thought they would do or be with the families, friends, and partners with whom they imagined they would spend their lives. He could still remember what it was like as they were preparing for the Nyx 23 mission. It had been the most thrilling time in his life, so filled with hope and anticipation. The entire reason that he had joined the department was so that he would be able to make a difference. Even though the program was designed primarily for research and recognizance, he had felt deep within him that it was going to give him the opportunities that he desired to really make a difference.

Nyx 23 had been the first chance that they had to do something truly impactful. They had done seemingly endless research and gone on a few missions, but none of them carried the weight and significance of what they had planned for the then-unknown and unnamed planet that they knew was harboring an illegal prison colony. This colony had been such a severe and blatant breech of the intergalactic agreements that at that time had only recently been made. Jonah had been one of the first people to start suspecting that the colony existed. The planet had seemed unoccupied, and according to the government and even the rest of the department itself, it was. In fact, when it was first found and identified as an inhabitable planet, some companies put in applications to receive permits to establish and build it as a tourist attraction. Jonah's department had been instrumental in tying these applications up so that they wouldn't be able to go through until after they made their mission. The last thing that they needed was for tourist companies to arrive on a planet that was being used illegally by a cruel and vicious species to imprison another.

Despite the severity of what was happening on what was now known as Penthos, and the horrors that they knew that they might face when they arrived, there had been such hope and even excitement when they prepared to leave. This was their chance. They were going to get to do something that not only helped others, but that changed the perspective of the entire galaxy. They might even be able to be the ones who decided how the planet was utilized after the prison colony was emptied and destroyed. Because so many of the original department hadn't believed what they were saying when they told them their suspicions about the prison colony, Nyx 23 was developed in secret, and the plan for the mission had to be made away from the rest of the department. At the time, the goal was to protect their plans and their mission from others who would be able to stop them. Now, though, he wondered if they had truly made the right decision by remaining so secretive. By concealing everything that they were doing they ensured that they were able to put the mission together and leave without interference, but it also meant that it took longer for anyone to take note of the fact that they were missing, and then once they did realize that the crew and the experimental ship were gone, they had little information to go on in an effort to find them. Even the skeleton mission control that remained on Earth only knew that they were traveling to the planet now known as Penthos. They would have no way of knowing what happened to them, just as the crew itself had no way of imagining what they would encounter when they left Earth behind.

Remembering the hope and determination that had filled him in the days leading up to their mission reassured Jonah that he had made the right decision staying on Earth rather than returning to Penthos. It wasn't a decision that he made because he was afraid or that he didn't want to be involved in the conflict that was threatening not only his kind but those who had freed them from the horror of the Covra. Instead, this was a decision that was made by a heart and mind still linked tightly to the past. It was as if he was getting another opportunity to make this right. He couldn't save the lives of those who had already been lost, but he could save their memories. And for those who were lingering on, and who they had met along the way, he might be able to save their futures.

THE ANGER COURSING through Ryan was so intense that he couldn't even bring himself to express the violence that burned in his veins. He sat in his chair, his hands gripping the arms until his knuckles ached and the wood cut into his palms. He could sense the presence of the Valdician man standing close behind him, but he didn't turn to look at him, and the creature said nothing. Finally, he brought enough control into himself that he was able to speak.

"How could they allow them to leave?" he asked.

"They fought," the Valdician replied.

"There should have been chaos," Ryan said. "The anger and the energy of the battle should have made the Klimnu insatiable. The Denynso wouldn't have been able to tolerate it and they would have killed him. All hell should have broken loose."

"They're healing him," the Valdician said.

"Healing him?" Ryan asked.

"The Klimnu is nearly whole again. The Denynso healer has been working with him."

"That would be excruciating."

"I suppose after what you've put him through, he was able to tolerate it."

"Reprogram the survivors," he said. "I want full forces on Penthos. Maxim and Kyven must be destroyed."

There was a moment of hesitation and Ryan could feel that the Valdician was trying to come up with a way to tell him something. Ryan's grip tightened on the chair further and he felt his heart pounding even harder in his chest.

"Kyven is no longer on Penthos," the creature said. "And there are no survivors to reprogram."

"What do you mean?" Ryan asked.

"The ship was able to escape from Penthos."

"How is that possible?" Ryan roared, the control that he had been able to maintain shattered by this revelation. "Their ship was sabotaged. How would they be able to navigate it?"

"The one they call Rain is from Nyx 23. She remembers the first attack and was able to overcome it. They headed back toward Uoria."

"They've gone for reinforcements," Ryan said.

"We believe so," the Valdician said. "They brought those who had been wounded in the battles with them, including Kyven."

"And there are no survivors from the battle when they left the laboratory building?"

"There were survivors," the Valdician clarified, "but they

didn't get back inside the building. Pyra and his followers took them and brought them to the transportation bay with them. I can only assume that they are on the ship headed for Penthos now."

Ryan began to laugh, the sound bubbling between his dry lips so that they cracked, but the pain and faint taste of blood only made him laugh harder. The sound filled the space around him, reverberating off the walls. The Valdician didn't react. He stood completely still in his place by the door until the maniacal laughter stopped.

"They think that they are so powerful being able to escape, but they are running scared. They are so terrified that they have to go gather up as many others as they possibly can just to try to stand up to us. They are desperate and they have only seen a few of the army. When they are faced with the full forces, there is nothing that will bring them to victory, and it will be all the sweeter that we can destroy all of them at once and leave their bodies to be forgotten on Penthos forever." He paused and laughed again. "At least those that I don't want to use for myself."

"What instructions should I give to those still on Earth?" the Valdician asked. "Should I prepare them to go to Penthos?"

Ryan thought for a few moments, then shook his head.

"No," he said. "Send them to the other facility. When the battle on Penthos is over, there will be a lot of work to do and I want to be as prepared as possible."

"Very well, Sir," the Valdician said.

Ryan heard the creature leave the room and settled back into his chair again. For days, he had been staring at the same wall and now the surface seemed to be changing, the plain white surface seeming to swirl into color as it formed the images that inhabited his mind.

4

The music was still blaring around the small lounge, fueling the celebration for Bannack and Loralia's tying ceremony that was still going strong even long after the couple had slipped away. Rilex felt like he might have been the only one who had noticed that they left. The others were too invested in enjoying the party, lost in the music, dancing, and delectable food that turned the ship's lounge into an experience that was more festive than anything that Rilex had experienced since he left his own stream. The music around him was just as unusual. It was like nothing that he had ever heard and he wasn't sure that he was enjoying it as much as the others.

Rilex stood toward the back of the lounge, watching the celebration as it continued on in front of them. They laughed and danced, savoring the treats that Ty had created as they celebrated the union between Bannack and Loralia. The longer that he watched them, however, the more he wondered if it was only the tying ceremony that had filled them with such mirth and excitement. While he knew that all of them, particularly those who knew and loved the couple, were excited and happy to see the ceremony, and were touched by the lovely surprise that Bannack had created for her with the help of some of his friends and Loralia's father, he felt like it wasn't just their union that was keeping this party going for as long as it was.

According to those who had already made the journey, they had only a matter of hours between leaving Earth and arriving on Penthos where they were to reunite with the rest of the group and face off against the hybrids and Valdicians on the battlefield. This brief time would have been better used sleeping, eating, and restoring their minds and bodies than it was in the loud, energetic party. Even knowing this, though, Rilex still hadn't left the room. It was like he was drawn to the room, kept in place by the energy of the people who filled it. He knew that he should be resting. He should be eating the nutrient-dense rations that they had brought with them from the emergency chambers. He should be trying to prepare his mind for what they were going to face when they reached Penthos. Yet he couldn't bring himself to pull himself out of the protective, reassuring barrier that the party seemed to create. They weren't just celebrating the love and union of the Denynso warrior and his mate. They were also celebrating the very fact that they had made it onto the ship. After the torment and fear of the laboratory building, they had made their way out and though they were now on their way toward what was likely to be an even more challenging conflict, it was a step to have come this far, and one that filled them with excitement and joy.

Even as he was watching those around him dancing and enjoying themselves, there was something missing for Rilex. He hadn't seen the hybrid woman who he was so drawn to since they had gotten to the celebration after the tying ceremony. Though she had been there during the ceremony, and walked alongside him to the adjoining lounge were Ty, Jem, Leia, and Samira had worked together to design the celebration for Bannack and Loralia, she seemed to have disappeared in the time since. He could understand why she might not want to be there. Even he had known these people for longer than she did, and with the life that she had had, she would have no way of understanding what was happening around her or why everyone was filled with the joy, excitement, and hope that the tying ceremony had given them.

The thought made Rilex wonder if the hybrid woman even understood the concept of love or sharing life with another person. This made his heart tighten painfully as the depth and extent of the pain and destruction that Ryan had caused became even more clear. The horrific physical conditions and torment that these hybrids suffered was awful enough. But, delving into the emotional suffering and loss that they had experienced simply by merit of coming into existence was intolerable.

Rilex swept his eyes across the lounge and felt his breath catch in his throat. As if his thoughts of her had summoned her to him, the hybrid woman stood just inside the door to the lounge, alone and looking around the room uncertainly. It was obvious that some of the women had taken her under their wings, showing her the tenderness and consideration that she so desperately needed. She had bathed carefully, washing the blood, dirt, and sweat from her skin and hair, and her hair had been brushed so that it lay thick and soft down her back. The front was pulled back away from her face, and when she turned to look to the other side of the room he saw that that portion of hair had been braided and styled so that it twisted around and in on itself before resting in the center of her mane. The dress that she wore was delicate, the long sleeves and layer that covered the soft pink fabric thin and ethereal.

She was breathtaking and Rilex felt himself pulled toward her. He couldn't resist her, even if he told himself that he shouldn't have these thoughts for her, that she would never be able to understand what he was feeling or that she was made to feel the same way. None of that mattered to him, he just needed to be close to her. Keeping his eyes locked on her, he crossed the room carefully. He didn't want to startle her, but the way that she looked around the room made him hopeful that maybe she was looking for him again.

He was a few steps from her when she turned back and their eyes met. Something close to a soft smile touched her lips and she glanced down as if unsure of what she should feel or even if she should be there. Before she could get frightened and leave, Rilex stepped up to her.

"Hello," he said.

She looked up at him and he saw a soft blush of color across her cheeks. It only worked to make her more beautiful and appealing.

"Hello," she said softly.

"You look incredible," he said.

Though the music was still loud around them, he kept his voice low, wanting to create a private space around them and show her that he was focused only on her. He wanted her to know that she mattered and that, for the first time in her existence, she had a voice.

"I don't understand why they wanted to do this," she said.

"Don't you like it?" Rilex asked.

She hesitated, but then nodded.

"I do," she said. "It feels wonderful to be clean. I can't tell you how long it's been since I was able to take a bath or wore clean clothes." She reached up and ran her fingers through her hair. "They brushed my hair."

"You are beautiful," Rilex said.

"Thank you," she said.

"Would you like to dance with me?"

He wasn't sure about asking her, not knowing if she knew what he was asking or if she would even be willing to accept his touch. She hesitated for a moment, looking around at the others.

"Is that what they are doing?" she asked.

"Yes," Rilex said. "They're celebrating."

"I've never danced," she said.

"That's alright," Rilex said. "It's not difficult."

He reached for her hand, carefully tucking his fingers beneath hers so that hers rested lightly against his skin. It was a soft, fleeting touch, but the light contact of their skin would be enough for him for now. He didn't want to push her, to attempt to force her beyond what she could tolerate in these first moments and days of freedom.

She relented to the touch, allowing Rilex to guide her a few more steps forward until they were just at the edge of the center area of the room that the others had taken over as their dancefloor. The woman stood still and Rilex stepped up to her. He rested his hands to her hips, taking his time with every touch so that he could gauge her reaction and be prepared to step back if he needed to. As his hands settled onto her, though, he could feel her relax beneath the touch. He took another step forward so that their bodies were only a few inches apart. After a few moments, the woman lifted her hands and let them rest on the fronts of his shoulders. Her hands were trembling slightly, but he saw less fear in her eyes and more soft, awe-filled questions as she began to explore thoughts and emotions that she could never have even fathomed.

5

———

"Ellora," Athan said as he stepped into the kitchen.

Ellora wouldn't turn around. She didn't want to face him right then or deal with anything that he might have to say. Instead, she focused on preparing food for those who had traveled from the distant planet to return to Uoria. Though she didn't want to know more about what they were facing on that planet or the plans that they might have for returning, she could see that they were in need of sustenance that would help them to recover from whatever they had suffered in the time that they were away, and prepare them for what they might need to do moving forward. She could only hope that she could somehow convince them that they needed to let this go, to stop the horror that had been carrying on for much too long.

"Ellora," Athan said again.

His voice made Ellora's muscles tighten. Though he had been a treasured and trusted part of her life, as close to a member of her family as she could ever want, he was also a painful reminder to her. Every time that she heard his voice say her name, she could only think of the night that he appeared at her door to tell her that her husband was gone. Aegeus had been precious to Athan as well, but as soon as she had heard this news, Ellora felt like something within her had closed. She wasn't able to feel the empathy that she knew that she should. She hadn't been able to reach out to him, to comfort him, or even to fully accept the comfort and support that he had tried to offer her. As much as she would have liked to rely on him more for herself, it was too painful. When she looked at him, she saw the eyes that had seen Aegeus after she had. When he spoke, she heard the voice that he had heard after he had heard hers for the final time. When he reached out to touch her, she could only think of the last time that she felt her husband's touch and didn't want to replace it with his.

"Athan, I don't want to talk about this," she finally said, knowing that he wasn't going to back down or leave her alone until she spoke to him.

"You have to," Athan said.

"Excuse me?" Ellora asked, turning toward him.

"You can't pretend it isn't happening, Ellora," Athan said. "You've spent years refusing to talk, and you don't have that option anymore."

"And who are you to tell me what I'm allowed to do or what I have to do?" she asked.

"There was a time when you would have trusted me completely," Athan said. "You would never have dreamed of turning me away or refusing to talk to me."

"That was different," she said, turning back to the pot on the large black stove and stirring it absently.

"How?" Athan asked. "How was that different?"

"That was when I knew that what was happening was inevitable and that there was nothing that I could do to make it any different. I knew what was going on and why, and could see the reason behind it."

"Could you?" Athan asked. "Did you really understand what was going on?"

"Of course, I did," Ellora replied, even though she didn't even trust the words coming out of her own mouth. "I always trusted that Aegeus knew what he was fighting for."

"And did you know what that was?" Athan asked.

Ellora poured the vegetables that she had chopped into the pot and sprinkled in some of the fragrant herbs from a canister on the counter beside the stove.

"He never gave me all of the details, you know that, but when he told me that he needed to go fight against the corruption in the Order, I knew that what he was doing was right. I knew that he knew what he was doing, and that no matter what he was facing, he was doing what was right for the Mikana, and for Uoria."

"And do you believe that now?" Athan asked.

Ellora fell silent. She wasn't sure what she should believe any longer. It had been so many years she couldn't remember everything that her husband had told her about the struggle that they were facing or what he wanted to accomplish when he went into battle.

"I don't know," she said. She looked at him sharply. "Why are you still a part of the Order?" she demanded. "How could you continue to serve the group that was so corrupt Aegeus went into battle against them and lost his life?"

Athan took a step toward her, shaking his head.

"You don't understand, Ellora," he said. "The Order is something far beyond each of the people who make it up. It is something that stretches beyond us, beyond the Mikana. It has always been and always will be, and until my death, I will serve it. I was chosen when I was a child. It wasn't my choice, and I don't have the choice of whether to continue."

"But you can betray them?" she asked coldly.

"What do you mean?" he asked, his voice falling softer now that she seemed to have broken through a barrier that had existed silently between her and the Order since he found out about the mysterious organization that her husband served with unwavering loyalty and devotion.

"You gave the vehicles to the Denynso and their team," she said. "You allowed Maxim, Ivy, and Kyven into the tunnels. Don't think that the members of the Order who remained here don't know what you did. They have already been here to question me."

"What did they ask?" Athan asked.

"They want to know where you are," she said. "They want to talk to Maxim and Kyven."

"Why would they want to talk to them?" Athan asked. "They aren't a part of the Order."

"I know," Ellora said. "That has always been one of the greatest comforts and reassurances of my life, but now I'm not as sure."

"Why?" Athan asked.

"Why weren't they chosen?" Ellora asked. "Their father, their grandfather, his father before him. They have all been in the Order. How could Aegeus's sons not be chosen?"

Athan shook his head.

"I don't know," Athan replied. "I always expected that if Aegeus had any sons, they would be accepted into the Order immediately. None of us, though, not a single one of us, knows how the Order is built. We don't know who makes the appointments or why."

"But how is that possible?" Ellora asked. "How is it

possible that none of you know who selects the members or determines what the Order does? I know that there is a hierarchy. Even Aegeus said that the corruption was in the upper levels of the Order. If it is that clear, how can you not know?"

"It isn't that simple," Athan said. "Yes, there is a hierarchy. There are those who are leaders within the Order and who are respected to guide and provide structure, as well as uphold the laws and regulations. Many of those were the ones who had become corrupt and who Aegeus wanted to eliminate. Even within that hierarchy though, it isn't the end. It's well-known within the Order that there is more than just those on Uoria that we know and who we encounter in our operations. I can only assume that it is those who we never see who make the decisions."

"They didn't choose Maxim and Kyven," Ellora said, starting to feel desperate and worn. "They left them alone. Why do they need them now? What could they possibly want with them now?"

There was something in Athan's eyes. It burned there, waiting to be spoken and yet pushed away.

"What is it, Athan?" she asked.

"Ellora, your sons are brave. They are stronger than you know. It's in their blood. They might not have been chosen by the Order, but that doesn't change who they are. From the moment that they came into existence, it is has been within them to do what they need to do to protect the things that matter to them, and to do what is right. I know you don't understand, but what they're doing right now is exactly what they should be doing."

"The war ended," Ellora said. "After the battle when..." her voice trailed off and she drew in a breath to calm herself and steel against the emotions threatening her control, "when Aegeus died, everything went quiet. I didn't hear about any more battles. It was done."

"It wasn't done," Athan said. "This has never ended, it just went quiet. It's come back now, stronger than ever, and it's Maxim who is leading. Even Pyra, the strongest and most powerful warrior in all the galaxy, has given his trust and loyalty over to Maxim. They are leading together. You should be proud of him, not resisting what he's doing."

"I can't lose anyone else," Ellora said. "There's nothing that could make me willing to offer up my sons."

"Even for the safety of the galaxy? Of the entire universe?"

"The galaxy can continue without me losing anyone else that I love."

The inexplicable emotion flashed over Athan's eyes again and Ellora focused on it. There was something there, something that he wasn't saying, but that she needed to know.

"What is it, Athan?" she asked again. "Tell me."

The man took another step toward her. It was a movement that was both comforting and intimidating. At once she felt like he wanted to be closer to her to provide comfort and reassurance, but also that he may be closing her in, blocking her in so that he could control her movement when he finally spoke.

"You haven't lost anyone you love," he said.

"How could you say that?" she asked, angered at Athan's words. "I lost my heart, my love, my life."

"You haven't lost anyone," Athan repeated. "Aegeus is alive."

His voice trembled slightly when he said it, and Ellora thought for a moment that she had misunderstood him. She had to have misunderstood him. There was no way that what she thought he had said could possibly be true.

"What?" she asked breathlessly.

"Aegeus is alive," Athan said again. "At least I hope that he is."

"What does that mean?" Ellora asked.

"Shortly before we left Penthos to return here, we found out that he is still alive, but I can't promise that that is still true. That's one of the reasons why it is so important that we get what we need and get back to the planet and the others as quickly as possible."

"I don't understand," Ellora said.

The revelation had overwhelmed her and she was feeling dizzy. Blackness crept into the edges of her vision and small points of light burst in front of her eyes. She felt herself shaking and the strength in her legs slipping away. Reaching for one of the chairs at the table where she had sat with Maxim and Ivy when they first visited, Ellora took a few steps across the floor. She dropped into the seat, but continued to grip the back to stabilize herself.

Athan lowered himself into the seat across from her and dipped his head down to look into her face.

"Aegeus didn't die during that battle. He was captured and brought to Earth to be used in experiments by a man named Ryan. He has been held captive ever since. Now Ryan is after the others, but Maxim and Kyven especially."

"Why?" Ellora asked.

"He is working to breed a master race of soldiers that have the powers and capabilities of every species he can find. He wants to take over Uoria and use his soldiers to then conquer the universe. Maxim and Kyven stand in his way. It is their destiny to unify the planet."

"How?"

Athan shook his head.

"They'll fight."

"My husband is alive?" Ellora asked.

"I hope that he still is," Athan said.

"Did you know?"

"No," Athan said. "I promise you, I didn't know. I thought that he died that day, just as you have since then. I had no idea what he was planning to do during the battle, or what happened to him after. If I had known that he was still alive, no matter where he was or what was standing between us, I would have found him, or died trying. You have to know that."

"I do," Ellora said, nodding. She took a breath. "And now it's our chance."

6

I vy felt butterflies fluttering in her stomach as she approached the small, low building at the edge of the village. She didn't know what to expect when she stepped inside. Maxim had described this building to her before they left, telling her that this was where she would find the care that she needed. He assumed that she would first go to Ellora and tell her of the pregnancy before she went to see the midwives, but Ivy hadn't been able to bring herself to have the conversation with her. Ellora seemed tense and on edge from the moment that they arrived, and Ivy hadn't felt ready to share the news with her. She had been wary of her since they met, though she had begun to warm to her, Ivy was still hesitant and she didn't know how Ellora would react to finding out that her son had conceived a child in a time of war. Ellora didn't even want her sons fighting. Ivy couldn't imagine how she would feel about her grandchild being involved even before its birth. She knew, though, that she needed to find out as much as she could about the pregnancy now, and perhaps then she would be better prepared to tell Ellora.

Taking another breath, Ivy glanced around to make sure that no one saw her standing outside of the midwife building, then gently knocked on the door. A moment later a woman who appeared many years older than Ellora opened the door a few inches and peered out. She stared at Ivy questioningly for a few seconds and then her eyes widened. She opened the door further.

"You are Maxim's partner," she said.

Ivy nodded.

"Yes," she said. "My name is Ivy."

"Is Maxim home?" the woman asked.

"No," Ivy said. "He didn't return with us." She noticed the woman's face change as a flicker of fear went across her face, and she held up a hand to reassure her. "He was safe when we left," she said. "He chose to stay so that he could continue to fight, but we needed to come back to Uoria. Before we left, he told me to come here. Are you Opaline?"

The woman nodded.

"I am," she said. "Does that mean..." her voice trailed off, but her eyes lowered along her body to rest on her belly.

Ivy nodded, not wanting to say it and risk someone being nearby and hearing her. She was still guarding the secret vehemently, holding it close as if it somehow kept her closer to Maxim. Protecting this secret was a form of connection between them, something special and precious that, at least for the time, was just for them. She knew now that she had to share it with the midwife. She needed to know more about the child that was growing within her so that she could ensure it was safe and healthy, and could protect it as best as she could.

Opaline's face lit up and she opened the door the rest of the way so that she could reach out and take Ivy's hand. She guided her into the building and shut the door behind her.

"Come with me," she said. "Let me look at you."

Nervousness filled Ivy as she followed the older woman through the front room of the building and into a smaller space toward the back. She remembered when Eden was pregnant and neither the Denynso nor the Mikana were able to help her because she was human. It wasn't until Rey, the king of the Mikana kingdom, stepped forward and confessed that he had assisted his mother and grandmother with human births that she had had the help she needed to bring Lysander safely into the world. The thought of what she went through made Ivy worry now. She didn't know if there had ever been a Mikana baby born to a human woman and what that meant not only for her pregnancy, but also for her child.

As they entered the smaller room, Ivy hesitated. Opaline turned to her and tilted her head quizzically.

"Are you alright?" she asked.

"You know that I'm human," Ivy said, part-statement, part-question. "Will that make a difference?"

Opaline shook her head, a knowing smile on lips lined by time and emotion.

"I have delivered many, many children. I helped Ellora bring Maxim into the world."

The revelation filled Ivy with a sense of peace and trust. It made her happy to think of the same woman who saw her love in his first moments being there for the first moments of her baby's life.

"Rey was able to help Eden when she gave birth," Ivy said. "He knew what to do when none of the Denynso did."

"And you think that he learned those skills alone?" Opaline asked with a bigger smile. "Come along, now. Lie down here and let's see what we can find out about this precious new baby."

Ivy nodded and took the few steps to the elevated bed in the center of the room. The room didn't have any of the equipment and machines that she would have expected to see if she went to the doctor during a pregnancy on Earth. She reminded herself that the midwives in the Denynso compound didn't have any of the equipment, either, and that even midwives on Earth often forewent the machines and equipment. The love that she had found in Maxim and the life that she was even still just beginning to build was nothing like she would have ever expected. She would have to change the way that she thought of everything and her expectations for the future in everything that she did, but as she settled onto the table and lifted her shirt to allow the midwife to see her belly, she knew that she was absolutely willing to do it.

Opaline came up beside the bed and looked down at Ivy's gently swollen belly. It seemed like it had gotten larger in just the short time since she had told Maxim, and Ivy knew that she wasn't going to be able to keep it hidden from the others for long. She resolved to tell Ellora after she left the midwife, hoping to share as much information with her as she could, and then find a time to tell the others. She didn't want the news to become a distraction to the others, but at the same time she also didn't want them to feel as though she were purposely concealing it from them because she didn't want them to know, or she didn't care enough about them to include them.

"Do you know how far along you are?" Opaline asked.

Ivy shook her head.

"I don't," she said. "Maxim said that Mikana pregnancies aren't the same as human ones."

"He's right," Opaline said. "They aren't. But that's

nothing to worry about. I'm sure that you will be just fine. Both of you."

Ivy glanced around again, still somewhat concerned about the lack of equipment even though she already knew that it wasn't there.

"Is there any way that you will be able to tell if the baby is healthy, or when it might be born?" she asked.

"You're worried that I'm not a doctor," Opaline said.

Even though the words were almost accusatory, the woman said them with a softness that showed her understanding and compassion.

"I'm sorry," Ivy said. "I just don't know what to expect. This is my first baby. To be honest, I never even really saw myself as a mother."

"Really?" Opaline asked.

Ivy shook her head, resting her hands on the sides of her belly as if to protect the little one growing inside from the words that she had just said.

"I've always concentrated on my career. It was just really getting started when I came here to assist my mentor, George." She gave a short laugh. "He actually wasn't too happy to see me. I had originally told him that I wasn't going to be able to come, but then I got the opportunity to, so I came to surprise him. Even after I came, I thought that this was just going to be a brief part of my life. I was going to finish up what I could do here, and then go back to Earth and keep going with my career. I wanted to eventually have my own laboratory and work on my own projects. It never occurred to me that there would be anything beyond my work."

"But then you met Maxim," Opaline said.

Ivy couldn't resist the faint smile that touched her lips at the mention of his name. He had been the most unexpected development of her life. Uoria had been nothing like she anticipated, but it had been discovering Maxim that had surprised her the most. She had fallen so deeply in love with him so quickly, and even though she had wanted to go back to Earth, she knew as soon as she met him that she would never be able to be without Maxim. Now she couldn't even imagine leaving Uoria permanently. She could easily adapt to life on Uoria and even continue to do more research. He, however, would never be able to live happily on Earth.

"I did," she said, "and I love him more than I could ever explain. It is only because of him that I can imagine being a mother. I thought that my work would be the only thing that mattered to me in life, and now I know that I have more than that. I'm just worried that I'm going to do something wrong or that I'm not going to be ready when this baby comes.

"You don't need to worry," Opaline said. "I can see it in your eyes. You are made to be a mother, and as soon as this little one arrives, you will know what to do. It will come to you."

"But how do we know when it will arrive?" she asked. "Have you ever helped a human woman through a pregnancy with a Mikana baby?"

She knew that the question was futile. This was unknown.

"I haven't," Opaline said. "But I know enough of the signs for both to be able to care for you throughout the pregnancy and until you deliver. We'll have to be careful, but together we can bring this baby into the world safely and happily. Now let me examine you."

As Ivy began to undress in preparation for the examination, her mind wandered back to Maxim. She wished that he could be there with her. She longed to be back on Penthos with him. Even though he had made it clear that he didn't want her returning to the battlefield even when the others came back, she couldn't imagine staying on Uoria without him. Eden had fought alongside the men while she was pregnant and hadn't been questioned or stopped. Ivy only wished that the others would see her as strong as they saw Eden, and as capable of taking care of herself and her baby while she continued to be a part of the efforts of the others. It was a thought that she would never have had before she left Earth for Uoria, or even in her first weeks on the planet. Being a part of a war wasn't something that she would have ever envisioned herself doing, but now all she wanted to do was be back on Penthos with Maxim, fighting to protect the family and the life that had become all that mattered in the world to her.

7

———

Maxim tucked his arms under Zyyr's and ran backwards with all of the strength and energy that he could build in his muscles. The sun was beating down on his back with vicious intensity and he could feel it searing through the fabric of his shirt painfully. The heat brought sweat down his face that stung in his eyes and mixed with the blood on his arms and chest. He could feel Zyyr trying to help him get him across the deep, stinging sand. The warrior's heels dug into the sand, forcing him backwards a few inches for every step that Maxim took.

He could still hear the voices of the hybrids that were marching away from the site of the brief but intense battle that they had just waged. The few that had survived were carrying the wounded, but Maxim hadn't seen any compassion in the assistance that they gave. It was almost as though they were already dead and their fellow hybrids were merely bringing them back to wherever they had been sleeping on the planet. Maxim got through the gate to the inner compound and released Zyyr so that he lay back on a cushion on the floor.

"Are you alright?" he asked.

The warrior nodded.

"I'll be fine. Thank you for getting me in here."

"What hurts? What did they do to you?"

"My leg," Zyyr answered. "I think it might be broken. One of them had a club that they hit me with. It brought me to the ground and took the wind out of me, but I don't think that there's anything serious but the bone. That will heal."

"But it will take time," Maxim said. "We need to stabilize the bone and then you're going to have to rest. You aren't going to be able to fight anymore."

Zyyr struggled to sit back up, an almost frantic look on his face.

"I have to," he said. "Nylek, Kyven, and Athan are already gone. There aren't enough of us left to help you if there's another attack. You can stabilize the bone, but I have to fight."

"Zyyr," Maxim said. "You can't. There's no way that you can safely go back out onto the battlefield. You will be an easy target. I know that you want to fight, and I appreciate your dedication, but I have to make sure that you stay safe as well. Ryan wants to destroy all of us. We can't give him the satisfaction of making that easy for him by putting ourselves in danger. The others are coming. We just have to stay strong and resist the hybrids until they get here."

Finally, the warrior seemed to relent. He rested back, his eyes closing and the color draining from his face as if the pain of the injury to his leg was settling in. Maxim rushed further into the building to get the bag of supplies that they had kept from the ship when the others left. He brought it back into the front room and called out to Lynx and Elise. When they came into the room, he gestured for them to come closer. He knew that speaking too loudly would only make the warrior feel more anxious, which could worsen his pain and even make it more difficult for his body to heal properly.

"I need you to find something that I can use to stabilize his leg," he told them. "Then find me as many rags as possible. If you can't find them, bring anything that you can. We need to get the bone in place and secure it so that it can start to heal. I'm going to give him some of Ciyrs's serum to relax him and ease the pain, but it will only last for so long, so we need to hurry."

Lynx and Elise both nodded and hurried out of the room. He knew that both were still struggling being away from their mates and he hoped that helping him care for Zyyr would distract them and help them to keep moving forward. He was particularly concerned about Elise. This was not her world, not the life that she ever thought that she was going to live. She had already been away from Azra for longer than any of them had been separated from their partners, but she had also been thrust into a war that she didn't understand. As they had said when they arrived on Penthos, however, she was the mate of a Denynso warrior. It had been her decision to give her heart to him, and when she made that choice, she was also choosing to give over her life to the Denynso way. By being with them on the journey and having the strong connection with Azra that all Denynso had with their mates, she had made herself a part of the conflict and she had little choice but to go along with it.

Maxim could see the fear and worry in her eyes, but he also knew that she was stronger than she thought. She had already proven herself in the ship and during the first battle with the hybrids. Though he knew that she wasn't going to be like Eden, Leia, or Zuri, or even like Ivy, anything that she could do for them would benefit them and would make

Azra proud. All she needed to do was believe in herself and what she was capable of doing.

Reaching into the bag again, Maxim withdrew a small battle of the calming serum that Ciyrs had created and opened it. They had very little to last them for as long as they were on Penthos, so using it had to be cautious and thoughtful. The pain that Zyyr was clearly in, however, justified the use of as much as he needed, at least through the challenging and potentially excruciating process of putting the bone back into place.

"Are you ready?" he asked.

"Is Lila here?" Zyyr asked.

"I don't think that she should be here to see this," Maxim said. "Drink this."

His eyes moved down to Zyyr's leg, drawing in a breath as he looked at the bleeding wound created by the shard of bone sticking through the warrior's leg. The fact that Zyyr didn't know the severity of the injury was a benefit, and he didn't want his mate to see it and make the situation any more anxious. Zyyr nodded his agreement and allowed Maxim to pour the serum into his mouth before he settled back against the mat. His eyes were still closed and he seemed to tighten them as if squeezing them harder would prevent some of the pain that he knew was coming.

"Just relax," Maxim said. "You'll sleep for a while."

Even as he spoke the mixture of herbs seemed to be taking effect. Zyyr's breathing had become deeper and more even and the tension in his face was releasing. Maxim immediately went to work cutting away the bloodied fabric of Zyyr's pants to provide better access to the injury. He took a cloth and splashed as little water onto it from his canteen as he could while still dampening the surface. He didn't want to waste any of the precious and limited water that they had, but he knew that he had to get the wound clean. He was finishing wiping the skin around the injury when Elise and Lynx came back into the room. Lynx was carrying an armful of pieces of wood and Elise held long rags that appeared to be made out of one of the blankets that they had brought with them from the ship.

"You're going to want to pack that wound with some of the herbs," Lynx said when he saw the full extent of Zyyr's injury. "That will help prevent infection and get it to heal faster."

Maxim nodded and took a container of herbs from the bag.

"We don't have many supplies left," he said. "Maybe we should have kept more before the ship left."

"We'll have to make do for as long as we can," Lynx said. "Ciyrs will be here soon. Hopefully he'll be able to help."

"Hopefully he won't have a reason to."

Lynx and Maxim met eyes and then Maxim looked away, concentrating on spreading the herbs into Zyyr's leg. He couldn't let himself keep going along that train of thought. In this moment, he needed to concentrate only on what he needed to do for Zyyr.

Lynx handed him the first piece of wood and Maxim looked down at it. It appeared to come from one of the pieces of furniture that they had found in the building. Maxim placed the piece beneath Zyyr's leg, then accepted one of the rags from Elise. They worked as quickly as they could and soon Zyyr's leg was fully bound and properly supported. Elise left the room and came back a few moments later with Lila. She held another blanket in her arms and Maxim could see the streaks of tears still on her cheeks. Lila approached her mate's side and carefully knelt down beside him. She draped the blanket over Zyyr and tucked it around him. She had begun to cry again, but the tears fell quietly and she said nothing as she reached forward and ran her fingertips across his forehead, brushing a lock of his thick white hair out of the way.

Maxim stood and walked out of the building. Lila needed this time alone with Zyyr as much as he needed to have her with him as he tried to recover from his injury. Evening was falling outside by the time that he stepped out into the air and the intensity of the sun had dissipated so he didn't feel the pain of it on his back any longer. It was a relief, but at the same time it meant the darkness was growing around the compound that they had claimed for themselves. The darkness was the most dangerous time. When the night came, they could hear the hybrids swarming to the walls of the compound, standing outside with their drums, taunting them, but never trying to get in where they were.

Maxim almost wished that they would. This was not what he had expected when it came to warfare with the hybrids. They knew that these creatures had been bred specifically for the purpose of fighting, and Maxim expected that the clash would be fierce and continuous once it began, but that wasn't what happened. Instead, there were long quiet stretches in between the battles, and when the battles did occur, they were brief. They would descend on them and clash, but within moments they were leaving, dragging their wounded with them. There had been few casualties, and when there were, the survivors often left them lying in the sand until the next battle, then brought them with them much like they did the wounded.

Maxim couldn't help but wonder about this approach to the war. When they had first arrived on the shuttle and Ryan confronted them, the hybrid army had appeared on the horizon. Their numbers had been expansive and Maxim had assumed that they would send as many of them as they could with each encounter. As soon as the fighting had begun, however, the army has dissipated, leaving only a few behind to engage with them. It was almost as though they were toying with them, tormenting them to make the conflict difficult beyond the physical fighting. With each wave of battle, they were breaking them down further, sending in fresh soldiers to replace the dead and wounded so that they were always at their strongest while Maxim and the rest of the group were growing more tired and worn with each passing hour. He wondered if this was the way that Ryan had planned it, knowing that if there was one tremendous battle the hybrids may not be able to withstand the tactics of the Denynso, but that if they simply kept pushing, kept attacking in brief but intense waves they would be able to break them down until they were completely vulnerable.

The thought was infuriating. It only illuminated who Ryan was, demonstrating that he was cruel and weak in everything that he did. Maxim had to remind himself that the others were coming. It didn't matter what the hybrids did. Soon those who had gone back to Uoria would return with supplies and a bigger army, and those who had been on Earth would join them, bringing with them the most powerful of the warriors and new insights into Ryan and what he was capable of doing. All Maxim and those still in the compound on Penthos had to do was survive. They just had to linger on, keeping the hybrids back long enough for the reinforcements to arrive so that they could battle them face-to-face.

As Maxim thought, he found himself wandering deeper into the compound than they had been. When they moved into the compound after the ship had left, they chose the first large building that they found to be their shelter. It seemed that it had once been living quarters, filled with aging furniture and dilapidated remnants of those who had once lived on Penthos before Nyx 23 arrived. Now that he was moving further into the compound, however, Maxim was seeing more of what Rain had described to them. Her memories of the space that they had infiltrated in an effort to free the prisoners and eliminate those who had built the illegal, vile prison colony had been vibrant and detailed, and Maxim could see the skeletons of those memories now. After the more than one hundred years that had passed since they had walked this ground, the abandoned buildings had begun to dissolve away under the power of the sun and the stinging of the sand that rose up when the rare but powerful wind blew.

The memories that Rain had shared were on the very edge of his mind as he walked through the rows of buildings. Part of him wished that he could have seen what she did, had been there to witness the colony as it had been. Maybe he would have been able to see something that the others didn't when they arrived. Maybe he could have changed what happened. If he had, though, Nyx 23 never would have ended up on Uoria, the Denynso wouldn't have started the exchange program with Earth, and he never would have had Ivy. Nothing would have been the same. This was his chance. This was the time to resolve the past and protect the future.

A large building rose up in front of Maxim and he stepped up to the door. The wood was old and dry from the heat and the sun, but a thick lock was still in place, preventing him from being able to open it. Maxim took a step back and aimed a hard kick right beside the latch. The wood cracked and another kick splintered it, enabling him to push the door the rest of the way open. Stale, hot air rushed out and Maxim took a step back to let the years flow out and rejoin the breath of the planet. When he stepped inside he saw that he was in a building that was far more elaborate than the other buildings he had seen. The furniture was larger and held faded padding that was absent from the furniture in the other locations, and the walls of the front room held massive frames with what looked like the remains of artwork. Time, heat, and brutally dry air had shriveled the art, leaving only shrunken pieces of paper that became powder beneath Maxim's fingertips when he touched them.

Maxim continued through the building, moving toward a door on the far end of the room. When he stepped through it he found himself in what he could only guess was the office that Rain had described. Unlike anything that Maxim had seen before, this space seemed like a small fortress of its own. The furniture here was more severe, including the heavy desk that sat toward the far wall. Maxim approached it cautiously, unsure of whether the office was truly still slumbering like the rest of the compound or if there were traps just waiting to lure him in. Finally, he reached the side of the desk and touched his hand to the surface. It felt warm beneath his fingertips and it was almost as though he was able to feel the energy of the creature who once sat behind it. Maxim walked around to the back of the desk and pushed the large chair behind it out of the way, not willing to sit in the same place that once held one of the Valdicians that had been the root of all the horror that they were now facing. He crouched down to examine the desk more closely, discovering a large drawer along the front.

Remaining cautious, Maxim took hold of the pull at the

front of the drawer and eased the drawer open. There were stacks of papers, files, and books inside, seemingly protected from the severe environment of the planet by the desk. Unlike the art that once decorated the walls, the papers inside the drawer were still in good condition, the words on them clear and legible. Maxim pulled everything out of the drawer, placing it on top of the desk so that he could look deeper into the drawer. He ran his hand along the piece of wood at the bottom and felt his fingertips hit something hard in the back corner.

Drawing the object out, Maxim looked down into his palm. The faint light streaming through the single window wasn't enough for him to clearly see what it was and he was beginning to feel strangely vulnerable and exposed in the building, as if there was someone there watching him even though he couldn't see them. He stood and gathered all of the papers from the drawer into his arms, then went back through the front room of the building and out into the night. The uncomfortable feeling immediately dissipated and he looked up at the sky, scanning the expanse to see any sign of the ships coming back. The stretch of stars was still. He would have to continue to wait, at least for now, for the others to come.

Maxim made his way back across the open expanse of the compound quickly. He couldn't hear the hybrids outside of the stone wall of the compound, but the silence was nearly as unsettling as the sound of the drums that had become their constant companion. When he arrived back to the building where they had settled, he could see a slight glow around the edges of the windows on the side. He hurried inside and found Zyyr sitting up, his back leaned against Lila behind him as she cradled his head against her chest and ran her fingertips through his white hair. His face was still paler than it usually was, but there was a slight smile on his lips as his mate comforted him. Lynx sat on the floor a few feet away with Elise leaning against the wall across from him.

Tucking the papers and journals in his arms closer to him, Maxim reached up to adjust the makeshift curtains that they had created to block the windows. Though the hybrids hadn't yet stepped inside the boundary of the compound, he didn't put it past them, and if they did he didn't want for them to be able to see the light that would betray their location.

"What's all that?" Lynx asked when Maxim turned around.

"I'm not sure," he answered. "Where's Avery?"

"He's in the back room," Lynx replied. "I think he may be sleeping."

Maxim nodded and settled onto the floor. He wasn't sure why, but he didn't feel ready to share the information that he had discovered with the human pilot of the ship that had brought them to Penthos. Though Avery had offered his assistance to the rest of the crew when they confronted him, he had still hidden in the panic room when he knew that the ship was going down. It was what he had been taught when preparing to pilot what he thought was a leisure trip, but the fact that he had done it, leaving those who were aboard at the mercy of the Valdicians that took over the ship soon after they left Uoria made it difficult for Maxim to trust the man completely. Avery had promised his service to them, and even commanded Elon, the human medic from the ship, to cooperate with the crew after the women found them hiding away, and Maxim had accepted it willingly. Despite this, though, he couldn't just consider this man one of them, a true part of what they were going through. The other two men had gone to Uoria with the others to make sure that the injured handled the journey safely. For now, Avery would have to remain on the outskirts of those who had remained behind. He would share with him what he could, but there were things that Maxim knew that he needed to keep close until he felt ready to make them known to the still-unfamiliar man. Even he didn't know what these papers held and he would wait until he did to make decisions about how to move forward with them.

Maxim placed the stack in his arms onto the floor and divided it into loose papers, files, and journals. The division was primarily arbitrary, achieving little but giving him some sense that he was doing something. The truth was he didn't know what he should do with what he found in the drawer in the office. Finding them had made him feel as though he were in a strange position. He was still in a moment of potential, not knowing what discoveries might be contained within those papers. As long as that potential remained intact, there was still the chance that he would be able to use it to make a difference in what was happening around them. As long as he left the papers unread and the journals unopened, he still had the hope that he had found some form of valuable information tucked away in the desk, waiting as the decades slipped by to be found so that he could use it to resolve the chaos that had befallen the planet again.

Everything would change the moment that he opened the journals, rifled through the files, or read the papers. Once he delved into them, he would know what he had found and if they made any difference. The potential would be gone and he would have to face whatever it was that he found hidden away in those words, even if they meant nothing to him. Even if they meant nothing to the planet, or the war, or the people who had already suffered so much on the dusty, searing surface of Penthos had had returned for vindication.

Maxim took one of the loose papers first, scanning his eyes over what looked like a list of names. He picked up one of the journals and opened it. He had flipped through several pages when he slammed his hand to the open page, his heartrate increasingly slightly at what he saw.

8

———

Rilex barely even heard the music around him as the woman gradually relaxed more and more in his arms and they danced at the edge of the others. Everything around them disappeared and he only cared about the strange but beautiful creature that he held close. Soon it seemed like some of the others were starting to drift out of the room, ready to take advantage of the time that they had left on the journey to get some rest. The woman stepped back away from him and glanced down at the floor as if she didn't want to meet his eyes. He didn't know if she was embarrassed by the closeness that they had discovered, or if this was something that she had been taught, a lingering reminder of the regimented, torturous life that she had led until they found her. He could only hope that it was the former. Time would make their interactions easier and more comfortable for her, but he didn't know if she would ever be able to get over the scars that were left from what she had gone through when she was still under the control of Ryan.

"I should go," she said so softly Rilex almost didn't hear her.

"Why?" he asked.

"People are starting to leave."

"So?" Rilex asked. "I'm still here. I'm not going anywhere. Unless you want to go somewhere."

The woman looked slightly startled.

"Where?" she asked.

There was nervousness in her voice that made Rilex's stomach turn. He wondered how many times she had been told where to go, and how often it had gone horribly for her when she went along with the command. He slid his hand down along her arm until it rested against hers, again not latching on or forcing the touch any further than she wanted it.

"You are safe with me," he reassured her. "I might not know what will happen or what we are going to be facing when we reach Penthos, but what I can promise you is that I will do everything in my power to protect you. You will be safe when you are near me and I will never put you in a position to get hurt again. I just meant that we could go to one of the lounges if you wanted to spend some more time together. If you would rather just go to one of the bedrooms by yourself to rest..."

"No," the woman said, cutting him off. "I'd like to go to the lounge with you."

Rilex smiled and nodded. He could feel her hand close slightly around his, not quite holding it yet, but transferring more of her touch to him than before. They started out of the room, leaving behind the remnants of the party that was still going on, and headed toward the nearby lounge. As they stepped into the lounge Rilex tried to imagine what the room would have been like if they had been on one of the leisure cruises that this ship was used for. He knew that it was designed to use for any type of transportation and had been used frequently for transport of researchers and teams between planets, but there were characteristics of the ship that made it clear that its purpose was not purely academic. This room had obviously been designed for comfort and relaxation, not something that would be a priority when it came to a school, scientific, or military mission.

As they walked further into the room to stand by the massive window that covered nearly the entire wall, Rilex imagined the happiness of those who would stand in this very position when they were on vacation, gazing out into the open space without a worry or a concern marring the view. It would be purely luxurious, the only thought in the mind of the person standing there likely being whether they should stand there for a few minutes longer or return to their room to sleep until whatever pleasures awaited them the next day. That thought made him wonder about the passenger pods and if any change would be made for those who had paid the premium price for one of the trans-galactic journeys rather than boarding the ship for work. Though they were fairly comfortable, he couldn't imagine them being the only place for sleep for those on the trips that could last weeks at a time.

"What are you thinking about?" the woman asked.

Rilex chuckled in embarrassment. He hadn't meant to lose himself in the thoughts that were running through his mind and forget that he was standing there with her. He turned toward her and gestured toward the window.

"What do you think of all this?" he asked.

Her eyes narrowed at him.

"What do you mean?" she asked.

"I was thinking about what it would be like to go on a vacation, just to be so peaceful and carefree."

"A vacation?" the woman asked.

Rilex realized that it wasn't a word that she would have any reason to know.

"It's when people travel just for fun. They go somewhere and relax, spend time with their loved ones, see things that they don't see when they're at home."

"I can't even imagine something like that," she said.

"Neither can I," Rilex said with another soft laugh. "I never took one."

"Can I ask you a question?" the woman asked.

Rilex nodded and looked at her.

"Of course," he said. "What would you like to know?"

"What are you? I mean, how did you get here?"

She seemed flustered and even embarrassed by the question, but Rilex understood. For someone who was created like a product rather than crafted out of the love two people shared, it was a completely normal and expected concept that she would wonder at the origin of others she encountered.

"I came here by accident," he told her. "I traveled through a portal in my home and ended up on Earth."

"Couldn't you just return there?" she asked. "Didn't you know how to?"

"No," he said. "It wasn't just that I had traveled to another place. I was many, many miles, but also many, many years from the home that I knew. Though I knew that it was possible because I had been doing it my entire life, it wasn't something that anyone here understood. I couldn't tell anyone what had happened and had no way of reaching out for help. I was stranded. I had no choice but to just assimilate and start a new life here."

"You said that you went through a portal," the woman said. "Why couldn't you just go back through it?"

She was asking the question in a way that told Rilex that she didn't truly understand what he was telling her or even what she was asking, but that she was trying. He wanted to encourage her, to reassure her that she was allowed to use the new freedom of thought that being away from the facility afforded her.

"Unfortunately, it doesn't work that way. The portals don't just go from one place to another and back. I'd never used the one that I did to bring me here, and I didn't know where it would bring me if I attempted to go back through it. There was a chance that it would bring me somewhere that I still didn't know and didn't know how to leave. Some of the places that the portals bring are extremely inhospitable. My only hope was that one day those from my stream would figure out what had happened to me and come for me. I settled in and started a new life here while I waited."

"And they never came."

It wasn't a question, but a statement, an illustration of her immediate, resigned reaction to any situation. No matter what was happening, or what the possibilities that the situation held, she was quick to believe that nothing good could come out of it. She would never believe that there was hope, even after she was rescued. As much as he didn't want to consider it, he knew that deep within her, she was likely still scared, still worried that at some point she would be back in Ryan's possession and that her life would be even worse than it had already been.

Rilex took a half-step toward her.

"They did," he said. "It took far longer than I expected, but they came. The son of my best friend, the man who I was trying to help when I went through the portal, ended up here with a human woman who traveled through the portals."

"But you didn't go back with them," she said.

He shook his head.

"No. I could have. They offered to bring me back, but I chose to stay here."

"Why?" the woman asked.

"I had work that I needed to do here. It had been so long, I had made a life here. I was accustomed to it. Everything back in my own stream had changed so much, I didn't have my same place there any longer."

She shook her head and turned her head to look out of the window at the blackness around them.

"I would have gone back," she said. "If I had a home somewhere, nothing would keep me from it."

"I did have a home," Rilex said. "I had two homes. My home there, though, wasn't the same as it had been. I wouldn't have been able to just go back and keep going as if I had never been gone. I had a home here. Over the years I had learned to live here and had been doing important work that would ensure the home where I was born and the home I had chosen were protected and wouldn't be destroyed."

"Destroyed by who?" the woman asked.

Rilex felt a chill roll down his spine. He wished that he hadn't said that. He didn't want to explain any of this. It was something that he had put behind him and now that he thought there was a chance that it wasn't fully behind him, he was terrified. Putting voice to it would only make it real, and he wasn't ready for that. Instead, he tucked a finger beneath her chin and turned her face toward him.

"Have you chosen a name yet?" he asked with a smile.

She shook her head.

"I asked you to choose one for me," she said.

"Why?" Rilex asked. "Don't you want to decide what others call you?"

"Does anyone choose their own names?" she asked.

"No," Rilex said, "but you aren't just anyone."

"I know," she said, "but I don't know if the words that I would use to describe myself would be anything I would want others to call me. You choosing something for me would let me know how you see me, and how others might as well."

It was a bold and forward request, but one that Rilex felt honored to accept. He could feel himself drawing closer to her, something within her calling out to him at just the sight of her and the feeling of her presence near him fulfilled an ache that he had likely always had but had only just come to know. He wanted to reach out and pull her into his arms again. He wanted to touch her skin and feel her heartbeat. He had to be patient, to take his time and give her time and space to grow and learn to be herself within this new and strange context of life.

"There are so many things that I could name you if I wanted to describe you," he said. "I could call you Beautiful, or Wonderful. I could reach into my heart and my past and name you Starlight. But none of those would honor you properly. You deserve a name that is yours and yours alone."

"And what is that?" she asked. "What will you name me?"

"Severine," he said without hesitation. "It means traitor."

It was a word that had stayed with him after it fell so bitterly from the lips of the other hybrid on the battlefield at the University. He had meant it as a cruel and vindictive insult, but the truth was that it was the kindest thing he could have called her.

"Severine," she said, sampling the feeling of the name in her mouth and its sound in her ears.

"When he called you that, he embodied you like nothing else could. You were everything that you were trained not to be; strong, courageous, powerful in your own right. To be called "Traitor" for the rest of your life will be a lasting reminder that you saved them all."

9

Jonah put the file in his hands aside again and picked up another one. He felt like he had gone through each of these files a thousand times already, but no matter how many times he looked at them, he still didn't understand what he was seeing. The information contained within them didn't make sense. He remembered the examination that he had undergone prior to the mission very clearly. He knew exactly what they had gone over with him and the tests that they said that they performed, yet the information that was contained within the files didn't correspond to what he remembered. Some of the tests and vitals that they had done weren't accounted for, while others that they didn't do were recorded with details that he knew hadn't actually been taken.

He put the file down and opened another, laying it beside the other so that he could compare them side-by-side, then opened his own and reviewed it against the others as well.

"I just don't understand," he muttered to himself. "The

height and weight are off. Not by much, but they're still wrong. Why would they do that?"

He read through the test results again.

"I know that I didn't have this test, but there's results."

The sound of his own voice in the silence of the room was uncomfortable and he fell quiet again. It was like just hearing himself talking without the benefit of someone responding underscored the fact that he was largely on his own. As soon as that thought moved through his mind, he knew that it wasn't accurate. Though there were others who were still in the basement with him, he knew that this journey that he was taking, the path that he was on as he tried to unravel the mystery of the files was his own. None of them knew what he had been through and wouldn't be able to help him. He wouldn't ask them to. They had gone through enough and were facing their own troubled and complicated journeys moving forward. They had already been forced into a war that meant nothing to them. They didn't need another fight that wasn't there placed at their feet.

He ran his fingertips along the series of numbers that was supposed to be the results of a test that he remembered taking, but knew that they weren't the results that he had gotten. Jonah sifted through the rest of the files and pulled one out. He flipped it open and read the same results from it. After a few seconds, he closed the file and turned it to check the name on the front to make sure that he had chosen the right one from the stack. He had selected it because he distinctly remembered the day after he had gone in for his examination when he sat down for lunch with Brandon and discussed their test results. This particular test had been presented to them as largely experimental. It wasn't one that they had undergone before for any of their missions, but the doctor had told them that they needed to go through it now because of specific environmental concerns regarding the area of space where Penthos resided.

As with nearly everything else that had to do with the department, none of them had questioned anything that the doctor had told them that they needed. As he looked back on it now, he cringed at how pliable they were, how willing they were to simply go along with whatever was said to them, whatever was expected of them, without question. It was as though they never even thought about themselves and what they were actually giving themselves over to, they were too wrapped up in the idea of what they might accomplish or who they might one day be. Now Jonah knew that he would never be that trusting or selfless. He would never be able to simply agree with what someone said without questioning what that meant for him and how it might turn out if he went along with it. Though he was happy to support and assist those who had come to mean so much to him on Uoria, he did so with caution, evaluating each step and each order before he followed it.

Jonah reviewed the test results another time. It was as though he thought that if he looked at them enough, he would be able to make the results change so that they better fit with what he thought that they should say. He knew that they didn't properly record the results that he had gotten on the test, and also didn't correspond with what Brandon told him that he had received. Though he knew that there was always a chance that Brandon had lied about his results, Jonah knew that when he looked at his own file he didn't see the proper series of numbers. Even if his numbers did even vaguely correspond with his results, Jonah knew that there would be no reason for Brandon to lie about his own results. The true purpose of the test and what the results meant was something that was never revealed to anyone on the team. They only knew that they were undergoing a new, experimental test that would ensure that they had some undefined characteristic that ensured they would properly withstand the environment of Penthos. Since they had no understanding of what the results even meant, there would be no reason for Brandon to try to fabricate his own results.

It was obvious to Jonah that the results were changed purposely, but why? What would be the reasoning behind putting the team through a strange experimental test, telling them their results without giving any explanation of what those results meant, and then changing the results when they recorded them in their files, especially if those files were just going to be hidden away for no one to see? He stacked the files carefully and tucked them against the wall so that they wouldn't be disturbed and then gathered his bag and his lightstick and started back up into the abandoned medical ward again.

This wasn't the first time that he had entered the derelict hospital since the others left, but Jonah still didn't know what he expected, or even hoped, to find when he explored the examination room. The glow of his lightstick filled the empty hallway and he let it fall on each of the closed doors as he went. He wondered why they had bothered to fill the rooms with the useless equipment before sealing up the hospital. Why didn't they bring it out with them when they left the building for the last time? Or if they weren't ever going to use it again, why didn't they just leave it in place in its original rooms rather than taking the time and effort to divide it into the abandoned examination rooms and then close the doors, almost as though creating tombs for the remnants of the era?

Jonah's thoughts wandered again to the strange reality of

the abandoned hospital. He couldn't understand why the ancient medical ward was still there. It didn't make sense. The rest of the old University had been demolished, yet this, the most outdated and unusable building of all of them, had remained so that it could be used as the lost and forgotten skeleton of the new laboratory building. He wished that he could return to the buildings that he had spent his time in when he was studying and working at the University. Walking through the hospital had given him a taste of his previous life, yet reminded him blatantly and painfully of how long it had been. These were not the floors where he last stepped before he climbed onto the ill-fated ship, but those that were had long-since been destroyed. It was a sad feeling to think that he had walked along those hallways so filled with anticipation and even excitement, not realizing that it was the last time that he was ever going to see them. It was a foregone conclusion that within a few weeks, they would return and simply walk along the same path back to the department rooms. Instead, he had moved along that familiar path, the images that he was seeing passing through his eyes and into memory.

Without fully knowing why, Jonah turned away from the crumbling hallway and started back down into the basement so that he could go back up the stairwell and into the corridor above. He stepped out into the corridor and was immediately struck by the energy that filled the space. It was as if he could still feel what the rest of the group had felt when they were making their way down the corridor and out into the open space around the building. It suddenly struck him that he didn't really know what had happened to them in the time between them leaving him in the basement and them getting out of the building. He could only hope that it had not been as difficult as the last time that they were there. Ignoring the nervousness that made its way down the back of his neck and into his stomach, Jonah made his way toward the stairs that they had climbed to go through the laboratory building. He wove through the floors of the building, trying to remember what doors they had used, until he finally found his way back to the room behind Ryan's lab.

Jonah hesitated in the backroom. He didn't know what might be inside the room, if even Ryan himself could be waiting for any that might return. For a moment, he considered turning back around and heading back to the basement, but he knew that he couldn't. He had to go beyond just the basement and the medical ward if he was going to understand what happened. His hand felt almost electrified as he placed it on the doorknob to the lab and pushed the door open. As soon as he stepped inside he was struck by the cold, still feeling, and sharp, unnerving scent of the space. He looked around and knew immediately that they had not been the last ones who had walked through that room.

There had been chaos in the lab the last time that he had been inside. The conflict with Ryan had tossed the entire space into complete disorganization and left the surfaces covered with blood, chemicals, and other remnants. Now the entire lab was back in its original pristine condition. If anything, it was more organized and cleaner than it had been before. He could smell the cleaners used to wipe away all reminders of them and feel the chill of the temperature having been turned down to accommodate a delicate experiment.

The Valdicians had been here. They had come to the lab after the group left to repair what they had done and bring the room back into the condition that Ryan expected. Jonah couldn't imagine that they would have done something like that out of any sense of kindness or affection for Ryan. Instead, it was more likely out of a sense of responsibility, obligation, and even fear.

He walked to one of the tables and ran his fingers along the surface. It was cold but dry, telling him that the room had been restored well before, likely only briefly after they had captured Ryan. Most likely they had come into the room to free him and been commanded to fix the damage that had occurred, as if Ryan believed that he could pretend that it hadn't happened if he didn't have to look at it. He was leaning down to look under the table when he heard a slight gasp from across the room.

Jonah stood up sharply and looked toward the door. He hadn't thought to look at the main door to the lab when he first stepped in and now noticed that it was standing open a few inches, revealing a figure standing in the hallway just outside of the lab, a halo of golden yellow glow at its feet.

There was a tense moment when both stood completely still, aware of the other, but unsure of what to do next. Finally, Jonah took a step forward and lifted his lightstick up above his head to shed more of the light toward the figure so that he could see it more clearly. When it did, he could see that the figure was a woman, her hand rested on the door-knob. She looked both startled and confused, but unafraid.

"Hello?" she said.

"Hello," Jonah replied.

Her head tilted slightly and Jonah wondered if there was something about his voice that sounded different to the people of Earth a century after his own time and that had struck this woman strangely. She took a somewhat hesitant step toward him, crossing the threshold of the lab. Her hand slid across the wall beside her and her finger pressed into a dip on a silver metal panel. In an instant, the room filled with a blinding white light. After days with nothing but the glow of the lightsticks and the light from the small lanterns in the basement and the hospital, the illumination felt like it was exploding in his head. He grasped his temples, pressing against the pain that he felt in his temples and crumbling forward with the shock. It took several moments for his eyes to acclimate to the bright light and for him to be able to open them again. When they did he found that the woman had disappeared. He rushed around the table to the door and looked out into the hallway. He could see the faint remnants of her light moving around the corner at the far end of the corridor and felt an uncomfortable sensation in his belly, wondering who this woman was and why she had come to Ryan's laboratory in the middle of the night when the building was locked and no one else was supposed to be there.

10

Nylek winced as he made his way around the perimeter of the room, trying to convince his legs to move normally and willing the pain in his body to go away. The treatments he had received on the ship had effectively begun to heal his wounds, but not receiving a healing from Ciyrs had left him feeling weaker than he ever had this long after being injured, and he could tell that some of the gashes in his skin were still only tenuously healed. No matter what he was experiencing, however, he hadn't wanted to spend more time lying in the bed in the clinic. He felt like he had been trapped in a bed for longer than he ever had, and it made him feel fragile and vulnerable, things that he couldn't stand feeling. As soon as he was able, he had gotten out of bed and left the clinic, insisting that he go to one of the homes in the kingdom for the rest of the time that they were in Uoria. He would have preferred to be back in his own home in the Denynso compound, but he knew that the journey was too far, and by now nearly everyone who had remained in the compound when they left for Earth was now in the kingdom with the Mikana.

Elon and the Mikana doctors didn't seem confident that he would be well enough to return to Penthos with the others when the ship left, but Nylek refused to accept it. Until they had boarded the ship again and were gone, he wouldn't admit that he wasn't able to go with them. For now, he would keep walking, keep moving to start rebuilding his strength and encouraging his injuries to heal further.

The door behind him opened and he saw Mina step inside. She looked startled to see him out of bed and held a stack of blankets toward him.

"I brought these for you," she said.

Nylek looked at his mate, feeling his body and his heart burning for her. It had felt so long since he had left her behind in the compound so that they would be able to communicate with Creia while they were gone. He had missed her so desperately, but since he had returned to Uoria injured, she had seemed skittish and unsure around him. It was as if she didn't know if she should get close to him or if it might hurt him further.

"Mina," he said. "Please. Come here."

"I shouldn't," she said. "You should be resting. Without Ciyrs..."

"I don't need Ciyrs," Nylek insisted. "I'm healing just fine on my own. I just need you."

"You need to rest," she said. "Just get back in bed. Get some sleep."

He could hear the emotion and tension in her voice, and knew that she was struggling seeing him wounded after being apart for so long. Of course, he had been injured before, but that had been as a result of battles that she understood. She knew what they were facing and the dangers that they would experience while fighting. When he left Uoria with the others, though, she didn't know what he was going to encounter or what he would have to do. It was bad enough that he came back hurt, but she also knew that he hadn't returned with everyone else, and that the encounter wasn't over. His mate couldn't stop worrying about him because the situation hadn't yet come to an end and they had no way of knowing what else they were going to have to face.

Mina turned and started back out of the room, but Nylek followed her. He got to her in the hallway that led away from the bedroom and out of the house. Without saying anything, Nylek wrapped one arm around her waist and swept her up against his chest, crushing his mouth down on hers. Mina didn't resist but gave herself completely into the kiss, wrapping her arms around his neck and opening her mouth to allow his tongue to slip through her lips to massage against hers. The hesitation was gone, replaced by passion and need that told him his mate had missed him with the same fire that he had missed her during the time that they were away. He no longer cared about the pain that still lingered through his body. All he cared about was feeling her and reconnecting with her now that they were back in each other's arms, at least for the time.

Nylek led Mina back into the bedroom and kicked the door behind him. His mouth continuing to play across hers, he turned and lowered her to the bed. He stepped back and stared down at her as he peeled off his shirt and tossed it to the side. Mina stared up at him, her eyes widened in awe of the sudden kiss and her lips slightly swollen and red with its passion and intensity. He undressed as Mina watched him, revealing himself to her completely and purposefully. She watched him with a blend of emotion in her eyes. There was a powerful, slumbering hunger that he knew was reflected in his own eyes as well, but there was also something softer and more tender. Nylek could see her gaze settle on the lingering bruises and scars of his wounds, but she didn't wince or try to look away. Instead, she focused on them, following them like she wanted to know everything that he had gone through when he was away from her.

He could see Mina's eyes roving across his body, taking him in as if memorizing every inch of him, committing to memory the new injuries that had changed the landscape of the skin that she already knew so well. They had completed their bond years before, but his passion and love for her had never changed. He still craved her with every breath and felt the flutter deep within him when he thought of her. She was the greatest aspect of his life and the most precious companion he had and would ever know. He stepped forward and reached for the waistband of her skirt. He eased it down over her hips, revealing only the thin, gauzy panties that she wore beneath. Growling deep in his throat, Nylek removed the rest of her clothes almost frantically, tossing them aside as fast as he could. He wanted to run his fingertips over every inch of her and feel her smooth curves against him. When he was gone he had dreamed of filling his hands with the softness of her nearly every night. Now that she was stretched out in front of him, nothing separating them, he wanted to show her everything that had filled his mind in those long, dark moments.

Nylek forced himself to slow down. As much as he wanted her, it had been too long and he had wanted her too much for him to simply rush through and make it end too quickly. He reached forward and placed his hands on either side of her ribs, then ran his hands down along the deep curve of her waist. Applying gentle pressure, he ran his palms around the full swell of her hips and then up her belly onto her breasts. The warm, familiar lushness of her body filling his palms made his body tremble with anticipation of the pleasure they would soon enjoy. He allowed his thumbs and forefingers to gently squeeze her nipples, feeling them harden beneath them. Mina arched slightly into the touch and he saw her eyes flutter closed as her lips parted. She was no longer resisting him or trying to avoid the need that she felt for him. Instead, she was soft and compliant beneath him, just waiting for Nylek to guide her as he reclaimed his life and pushed aside the injuries to show her that he was still just as strong as when he had left her side.

He drew in another long breath to keep himself calm and slow. He had to constantly remind himself not to move too quickly, to let himself enjoy everything that was to come and to savor every second of it. Memories of the taste of her brought him to his knees at the edge of the bed and his hands to her thighs so that he could ease them apart. They parted easily and willingly, and Mina's body opened to him. Nylek could already see how wet she was and the warm, musky smell of her body was enough to drive him nearly to the edge of what control he had. She was ready for him, waiting for him, but he still wasn't willing to let this end yet. There was so much more that he wanted to explore with her now that he was back with her and they had nothing but time to explore and enjoy each other. This was purely about them and he had every bit of privacy to indulge himself in every detail that his beautiful Mina offered. It was a gift that he wasn't going to take for granted.

Resting one hand lightly on her belly to hold her in place, Nylek ducked his head down and drew his tongue through her folds, moaning at the taste of her as it filled his mouth and reached into him to begin fulfilling the empty ache within him. Mina gasped and reached down for him, but he eased her hand away from his head, wanting her to relax and simply enjoy the attention that he was giving her. He licked her again, pausing for a moment to flick the tip of his tongue across the sensitive pearl of flesh. It began to come forward with his coaxing, further intensifying the sensation that he was creating for her. Nylek brought his other hand down and carefully eased one finger into her body. He felt himself melt slightly at the softness of her hot, wet walls closing in around it, and pressed it deeper until the heel of his hand rested against her pelvic bone.

He moved his finger gently within her as he continued to trace through her core with his tongue. He didn't want to leave any of her untouched or neglected. Nylek applied slightly more pressure against her upper wall, exploring the pattern of ridges until he found the smooth, slightly softer spot that he knew would push her to the brink of her control. It was a spot that he had discovered in the long afternoons and blissful nights that they had spent together, and one that he loved to touch and nurture, bringing whimpers to her lips and tightening the muscles through her hips and thighs. He rubbed his fingertip onto it a little harder and heard Mina draw in a sharp breath. Her body was starting to tremble and he knew that her own control was close to shattering. Nylek rose up over her and took her hands in his. He pushed them back and pinned them on the bed on either side of her head. Mina gasped slightly, but he could see her chin lift and her mouth open as if seeking him. Continuing to exert every bit of control that he could, he slowly stretched out across her. Gradually their bodies met so that their skin melded and she was fully enveloped in him. Nylek slowly lowered his mouth back to Mina's and brushed it slowly across her lips. She whimpered softly and parted her lips further. He dipped his tongue briefly into her mouth, allowing it to glide across the inside of her bottom lip, seeking out his mouth.

Nylek lowered his mouth to hers and offered a deep, languid kiss. He could taste all of the kisses that he had missed while he was gone, all of the words that he didn't hear, and all of the moments that they hadn't been able to share. After a few moments, he ran his hands down her arms and along the sides of her body, then wrapped one arm around her waist so that he could pull her closer to his body. In one smooth, controlled movement, he rolled both of them over so that she lay on top of him. The new position caused the warmth of her core to nestle against his erection. It was a promise of what was to come and he could feel the intensity of his desire for her increasing even further. Nylek reached for her legs and tucked his hands around the backs of her thighs so that he could pull them gently and cause her to straddle him. Mina pressed her hands to his chest to push herself into a sitting position, putting her body on display just for him.

In that moment, it seemed that Mina had found her confidence and was no longer intimidated by his injuries or by the unknown conflict that he had experienced. Neither of them expected what had happened when they agreed to help Creia. Nylek hadn't been part of the group of warriors who had gone to Earth or who was still in the Mikana kingdom. When he agreed to travel with them as a connection between those on Earth and those remaining in Uoria, particularly the King and Queen, he expected the journey to be primarily exploratory. There was always the chance of violence any time that the Denynso were involved in anything. Their reputation as fierce and aggressive warriors extended throughout the universe, and they had fought countless species and battles. The sudden brutality that they encountered, however, had been far outside of what he thought that he was going to experience, and he knew that it had been horrible for Mina to relay the messages that he sent through her to Creia. She was a distant witness, knowing what was happening and yet separated enough from it that she couldn't do anything about it or even be completely sure that she really did know what he was going through. To tolerate it, she had built up a barrier, closing off the emotions that she had been feeling so that she was able to handle the responsibility that had been presented to her. It kept her locked away from him, unable to reach what she was really going through and commiserate with him for his own suffering.

Now Mina had seemed to break through the barrier that had been made in her mind. She had broken free of the distance that she had built up in her mind and was ready to connect with him fully again. She lifted her hips, moving them forward so that her hot, wet core slid along his hardened length. Reaching forward, she wrapped her hand around his cock and held it in place so that she could slowly roll her hips against it. The sensation was nearly overwhelming and he dug his fingertips into her hips.

"You're so close," she whispered.

Nylek nodded, biting into his bottom lip to keep himself from toppling over the edge.

"I could just slide inside you right now."

Mina leaned forward, causing the taut peaks of her breasts to brush across his chest, and brought her mouth close to his ear.

"Please," she whispered, the warmth of her breath trailing along the side of his neck.

Nylek turned his head so that he could claim her mouth with his. As they kissed passionately, their tongues tangling, he used one hand to adjust their bodies until the tip of his erection just settled against her opening. He held her hips more tightly and then lifted his just enough that the very tip entered her. They both drew in breaths and he could feel her trembling. Pressing herself back, Mina sat up again. The new angle allowed her to sink down onto him until her hips rested on his. Nylek groaned as their bodies completely melded. They both paused, the sound of their breath, audible in the silence of the room around them, and cherished the feeling of coming together again.

Mina sighed softly and began to move her hips. She rolled them slowly but deliberately, ensuring that their bodies never parted while still guiding his engorged cock to massage her walls. The slow, steady darkness that had settled around them and now sent shadows through the room felt like it was cradling them, protecting them from the world outside as they worshipped one another and gave thanks for the bond between them.

After a few moments of simply treasuring the sensation of being enveloped fully inside her, Nylek pressed a hand to the small of her back to stabilize her, and then sat up to tuck her close into his lap. He leaned forward to rest his mouth to the soft dip at the front of her neck, and then rested his head against the front of her shoulder. Mina wrapped her legs tightly around his hips and her arms encompassed him, one coming around his shoulders and the other cradling his head as he nestled into her neck. Though she was smaller than him, as a Denynso woman she was far larger than the human women who had come to Uoria and found their mates. In that moment, he was blissfully grateful for it. Her size enabled them to wrap their bodies around each other fully, melding to one another in a way that wouldn't be possible if she were much smaller. She felt strong and lush in his arms, yet sweet and feminine. They remained in this peaceful position for several long seconds. The closeness of their bodies enabled their breaths to synchronize and soon Nylek felt like they were truly one. He tightened his hips to press into her more deeply and she rocked her hips to return the sensation to him. Nylek needed more. He couldn't be satisfied with just this any longer. He slipped his hand in between them and pressed the pad of his thumb to her peak. He applied gentle pressure and began to create small circles.

Mina's pace increased slightly in response to the touch and he met each rock of her hips with a lift of his own so that he sank more deeply into her with each thrust. Nylek filled her completed, fitting into her body in a beautiful, perfect way that reminded him with each long stroke within her body that she was crafted specifically for him. He had waited for Mina his entire life and had known the moment that he met her that they were intended to be together for the rest of their existence. It was only her. It had always been her, and would only ever be her. Neither could ever love another and their lives would be forever designed around their devotion to each other.

Nylek could hear murmuring coming through her chest and he drove into her until they became louder, faster, and more desperate. Finally, she reached forward and her hand gripped onto his back. He felt her arch, her body squeezing down around him as she cried out. The sound of his name tumbling from her lips with such abandon broke every semblance of control that he had left. Nylek lifted her up with one final, impaling thrust and he felt himself pulse before he poured into her. Each of her tight, hard spasms milked him, drawing him further into her and pulling out the hot streams that filled her.

When they both seemed to have relaxed and calmed enough to move, Nylek embraced her and rolled her onto her back. He came down over her as he continued to slowly stroke into her to extend the delirious pleasure of the aftershocks of his orgasm that rolled through him. He stared down at her, his hand absently brushing along the hair around her forehead, and felt a smile come to his lips. There was nothing that he could say at that moment that would even begin to express everything that he was feeling or the gratitude that he had just to be back with her. Even if they weren't able to remain together for long, even if he was able to recover enough to get back on the ship and return to Penthos with the others, he had these moments that he could hold on to and think of when he was away. All he could do for now was watch as her eyes fluttered closed and the soft smile on her lips relaxed slightly. When she was fully asleep, he rolled on to his side and allowed himself to fall asleep, feeling as though he were able to really rest for the first time since he had been away from her.

11

———

Ellora felt the muscles in her jaw twitch as she opened the door to the war room and looked around at the weapons that her husband had compiled. She didn't know how long he had been collecting the arsenal or how long he had been planning the war that he had hoped would ensue after the battle, but now it didn't matter. Gone were her hesitations about the conflict that her children and the rest of Uoria was facing. Gone was the fear and the bitterness that had been controlling and guiding her for the years since she thought he died. This was for Aegeus now. She reached forward and took down one of the largest swords that she could manage. It felt heavy and meaningful in her hands, speaking to her in a way that she couldn't explain. Behind her she heard Athan come down the steps and into the hidden space.

"What are you doing?" he asked.

"What does it look like I'm doing?" she asked.

She lowered the sword carefully to the surface of a table and reached for another, working to systematically remove the weapons from the room so that she could bring them up to the house and prepare them for travel.

"Does this mean that you will support Kyven and Maxim now? That you won't stand in the way of the war?"

Ellora turned and shoved a sheathed blade into Athan's hands.

"I will never be able to get back the years that were taken from me that I could have spent with my husband and that he could have spent with his family, but I want to destroy whatever took them. If Maxim needs weapons and an army, then I will get them for him."

Athan nodded and accepted another sword that she handed him before stepping up to the wall and gathering several into his arms. She watched him carry them out of the room and heard his footsteps climbing the stairs back up into her house. Tears of fury were stinging in her eyes, but she didn't want to give into them. She had already shed enough tears after Aegeus disappeared. The time to cry was over and she didn't want to give the creatures that had stolen him even a second longer of the satisfaction of her tears. It was her time to fight.

An intense compulsion burst in her chest and she stormed out of the war room and up the stairs. Out of the corner of her eye she saw her husband's symbol and resolve dried the tears from her eyes and settled the beating of her heart so she felt completely calm and under control. She was determined in a way that she hadn't felt in so long. No longer was she living in a shadow or surviving just for the sake of Maxim and Kyven. The blood seemed to be running through her veins again and she was thinking clearly for the first time in years.

Without saying a word to Athan, she lowered the weapons that she had brought up from the war room to her kitchen table and then left the house, starting toward the barely-used hatch that Maxim and Ivy had used to emerge from the Order tunnels when they first arrived back in the kingdom. This was her time, her chance to stand up and show that she had the strength and the ability to protect her home, her family, and her husband, and that had to start with confronting those who put him in the position in the first place: The Order.

There was a time when Ellora would never had even considered entering the tunnels that ran beneath the kingdom and were the stomping ground of those chosen for the Order. She knew that she wasn't even supposed to know that the organization existed, and once it was known that Aegeus told her of the Order, she wasn't supposed to know anything of their operations. She had always followed that as closely as she possibly could. It was an honor for Aegeus to have been selected for the Order. Though she didn't know what the organization did or even why it existed, she knew that it was extremely selective and the fact that he had been chosen to join them was incredibly meaningful. She didn't want to do anything that would disrespect him or the others, or put the organization at risk.

Now, though, she no longer cared. It didn't matter to her that she was never supposed to go down into the tunnels or that she didn't even know what she would find there. If Ivy, a human woman who had been on Uoria only weeks when she arrived at the kingdom, could walk through them and emerge without harm, Ellora was confident that a lifetime in the kingdom and the strength and power of Aegeus in her heart would get her through. As long as she found the leaders of the Order and was able to confront them, she didn't care what else she discovered in the hidden, unspoken world beneath her feet.

Ellora took a breath and dropped down through the hatch so that she could climb down into the tunnel. The colored lights burst on above her and she felt immediately exposed, but instead of it making her feel vulnerable, it was as though the multicolored glow above her was announcing her arrival. She stalked down the tunnel, not knowing where it was leading. When the path turned or forked, she let her heart guide the way. Suddenly she heard fast footsteps and harried voices in the distance. Above her the light in the ceiling glowed red and she stood her ground, wanting for whoever it was who was coming toward her in the tunnel to find her. She wasn't going to hide. She wasn't going to apologize for her presence in the tunnels. It was their turn to explain themselves.

A moment later she could see the darkness ahead of her dissolving away as the lights in the ceiling turned on in sequence, announcing the approach of whoever was in the tunnel with her. She knew that they could see her light now and soon they would be able to see her face. Her fingers twitched and she wished that she had brought one of the swords with her. For now, the small dagger that she had tucked into her boot would have to suffice. The rhythm of her heart quickened, but not out of fear. She was beyond fear. This was excitement, a thrill at getting closer to a truth that had always been kept away from her and dangled just out of reach, though in the back of her mind she had hoped she would discover it.

The footsteps drew closer. They were only yards from her now and she knew that it was only a matter of seconds until they would see her face and know exactly who had invaded their private world. Ahead of her the light in the ceiling turned yellow and then white. Three figures came into view and she felt her stomach twist. They paused, not drawing near enough to trigger the light segment just ahead of her so that a bar of darkness remained like a wall in between her and the men now glaring at her across it.

"Ellora," one of them said. "What are you doing here?"

"Malcolm," she said, barely able to get the name past her lips. "You are a part of this?"

"Ellora, you shouldn't be here," Malcolm said. "You don't belong down here."

"Yes, I should be here," she said angrily. "I should have come down here long ago. How dare you keep this from me? How dare you not tell me?"

"I don't understand," Malcolm said. "Tell you what? You of anyone should know that I wasn't allowed to say anything to you about the Order or that I was a part of it. The only person who was permitted to let you know that he was a member was Aegeus."

"Don't you dare say his name," Ellora spat. "You are never allowed to say his name."

"I don't understand," Malcolm repeated. "Why are you so angry? Why did you come down here?"

"Why am I so angry?" Ellora asked. "My husband was bound to serve an organization whose origin he didn't know and whose purpose he didn't fully understand. He discovered extensive corruption among the hierarchy that was meant to be the most honorable and powerful of all Mikana, and when he fought against them, he was taken from me, from our children. I have suffered for years wondering what happened to him and trying to explain to boys who were rapidly turning into men why their father was just gone. I came down here to confront them, these creatures who claimed lives for themselves that never belonged to them, used them, and then tossed them away. I came down here to see what could possibly be so important that it would justify how grotesque the Order really is. Then I find that my brother has been a part of it all along."

"I couldn't tell you, Ellora," Malcolm said.

"Is that why you stopped talking to us? I married Aegeus and you just left my life. It was like you never even existed."

"It was just too hard," Malcolm said. "I hated having to lie to you. I knew Aegeus and it was too difficult to balance being in the same family and being in the Order together."

"So, you chose the Order," Ellora said accusingly.

"I had no choice. You don't understand."

"*You* don't understand," Ellora said. "Not telling your only sister who you really are isn't hard. What's hard is losing the love of your life. What's hard is raising two boys alone and hoping every moment that they wouldn't realize that they didn't have any masculine influence and lose all of what of their father was within them. You could have been there for them, Malcolm. You could have been there for Maxim and for Kyven, helped them deal with the loss of their father."

"You did fine on your own," Malcolm told her.

The comment was meant to be encouraging, but it only enraged her further.

"I shouldn't have had to!" she screamed. "I *never* should have had to."

"You don't understand," Malcolm said again.

"Then tell me," she said. "Explain to me what could possibly be so important about the Order that you could turn a blind eye to corruption, violence, and death."

Malcolm opened his mouth as if to respond, but no words came out. Instead, his eyes widened and seemed to focus on something over Ellora's shoulder. She began to turn, but she felt a hand clamp around her wrist and another clasp the back of her neck.

"What do you think you're doing down here?" a voice hissed into her ear.

Ellora fought out of the grip on her neck and turned, finding a man with a dark red mask standing close behind her.

12

———

"I'm so sorry that I missed that," Ciyrs said in his mind, transmitting the message to Elianna in his thoughts.

His mate was on the ship with the others while he had taken the vehicle that Oro and Jonah had brought from Uoria so that he would be able to take care of the wounded and the pregnant women during the journey. The strange car was traveling far more quickly than he had anticipated it moving, and they found themselves ahead of even the large transport vessel from the University. Being away from Elianna during this journey was difficult for him even though it was only for a few hours. He hated that they weren't near each other and that he had no idea what she was going through. Now she was communicating with him through their thoughts, giving him a harsh reminder that she was far away from him and that if something did happen, he wouldn't be able to protect her.

"It was so beautiful," Elianna said. "It was so unexpected. We got onboard and I think we all just kind of expected that we were going to spend the next few hours getting some sleep. At least the rest of them were, I knew that I was going to have to be in the infirmary with the injured."

"The injured?" Ciyrs asked.

He didn't know what she was talking about. The whole reason that they were in separate vehicles was that Pyra decided the most wounded and the pregnant women should travel in the faster vehicle with Oro and Ciyrs rather than trying to make it all the way to the transportation bay to travel in the larger ship. He knew that she was going to be offering support to those who were in better condition, but he hadn't thought that any of them were bad enough off that she would need to be in the infirmary throughout the entire journey. The thought made him uncomfortable, as though he was failing even further in his responsibilities.

"Pyra brought the hybrid survivors from the battle."

"What battle?"

"We encountered the hybrids and the Valdicians," she said. "There were injuries and we saw them dragging away some of the hybrids. All we could think was that they would be put through the same things as the ones that we rescued from the breeding facilities. They brought them to the ship and I've been working on healing them."

Ciyrs drew in a breath and reached into his bag for one of the bottles of water that he had brought with him from the emergency chambers. He longed for a sip of something cold after days of the warm, still water from the basement. He shook his head, needing to get the thoughts of the wounded who were now on the ship out of his mind. There was nothing that he could do about it right now and he had to trust in his mate that she would be able to use the skills that he had given her through his first healing with her and the methods that he had taught her to stabilize and heal them as well as possible until he could get there to help her.

"Why did he do the tying ceremony on the ship?" he asked, trying to redirect the conversation back to the ceremony between Loralia and Bannack that Elianna had contacted him to describe. "I know he had mentioned something about a tying ceremony when he first met her, but I thought that they would wait until they were back on Uoria to do something like that."

"I think that's what she thought, too, but something changed his mind. I was in the infirmary and Samira came in and told me that I should take a break and have a bath."

Ciyrs laughed, then glanced nervously at the women who had finally fallen asleep across the furthest back section of the vehicle. He didn't want to disrupt their rest, assuming that it had been a long time since any of them had really been able to sleep deeply, knowing that they were secure and safe.

"That sounds pretty amazing right now," he said.

The sound of Elianna's laugh in his mind was refreshing and brought a bigger smile to Ciyrs's lips.

"I have to admit that it didn't take a lot of convincing. I felt bad leaving the wounded just so I could take a bath, but they were resting and I knew that there wasn't much more than I could do for them in that moment."

"It's alright," Ciyrs told her. "You can't always think of others. Sometimes you have to think about what you need, too. You can't be a good healer if you don't. Did you enjoy your bath?"

"More than I think I have ever enjoyed a bath in my life," she said, then paused. "Well, no." She paused again and Ciyrs felt like he knew what she was thinking about in those moments of hesitation. "The first bath that I took after getting out of the Covra prison. That was the best bath of my life."

"I bet it was," Ciyrs said, wishing that he could rid himself of the thoughts of that dark, horrific time that lingered in his mind.

"Anyway," Elianna said, obviously wanting to get away from the thoughts just as he did. "After I took the bath, Eden brought me some of the clothes that I had with me for the wedding and told me to put them on. I don't know what I was expecting, but somehow I just couldn't imagine that they were going to bring me to one of the lounges and Loralia and Bannack would surprise us all with their tying ceremony."

Ciyrs laughed again, but he felt a tug of pain in his chest. He knew that that ceremony was one of the most important events in Bannack's life, and he hated to have missed it.

"I really do wish that I had been able to be there to see it," Ciyrs said. "I know that was really important to both of them."

"I know," Elianna said. "And I'm sure that they were sad that all of us couldn't be together, but it was something that they felt like they needed to do. It was amazing to see Azrael officiate for them. I know how hard it was for Loralia when she first found out who he was, but it's obvious how much he loves her, and she seems to be really growing close to him."

"That's wonderful," Ciyrs said.

Suddenly he heard a small gasp behind him. He turned and saw that one of the human women was writhing in her sleep, her face contorted slightly as if she were either afraid or in pain.

"What is it?" Elianna asked, recognizing that his thoughts had turned away from the conversation that they were having.

"One of the women," Ciyrs said. "She's restless."

"I hate to think of what they're going through," Elianna said. "After everything that they've already suffered, they shouldn't be traveling like this, and they definitely shouldn't be going somewhere like Penthos."

"I know," Ciyrs said, "but I understand why they wanted to come with us. Would you want to stay in the facility where Ryan kept them? I know that some of them chose to remain there with Jonah, but if it was me, I would want to be as far away from all of that that I could possibly get. I would always be afraid that Ryan would come back and that I wouldn't be able to get away."

"But you know that it is very possible that Ryan will show up on Penthos with the rest of the hybrid army. We could be bringing them right to the most dangerous place they could be."

"No," Ciyrs said. "Even if he does come to Penthos, they won't be alone. They'll be with us, and we'll protect them. I just don't know what will happen to them from there."

"I don't either," Elianna said.

He was about to respond when the healer heard the human woman let out a sharper, louder cry. He turned to look at her and saw that she was now sitting part of the way up, her eyes open and wide as she clutched at her belly. She took a gasping breath and looked up at him frantically.

"What's wrong?" Ciyrs asked the woman, speaking out loud now as he leaned across the seat where he sat to get closer to her.

"It hurts," the woman gasped.

"What's going on, Ciyrs?" Oro asked from the front of the vehicle where he was piloting. "Is everything alright?"

The woman groaned loudly and another of them woke beside her.

"Astrid," the second woman said. "What is it?"

"It hurts," Astrid said again.

"What hurts?"

"My belly," Astrid answered. "It really hurts."

"You can't be in labor," the other woman said. "You still have more than a month to go."

"What's your name?" Ciyrs asked.

The woman looked at him briefly before turning her attention back to Astrid.

"Zadie," she said.

"What's happening?" Ciyrs asked.

Astrid curled around herself, crying out again and wrapping her arms around her belly tightly.

"She seems to be having contractions," Zadie said. "But she shouldn't be."

"Why?" Ciyrs asked.

"What's wrong?" Elianna asked in his mind.

"One of the women may be in labor, but another said that she shouldn't be."

"Is something wrong with her?" Elianna asked.

Ciyrs repeated the question to Zadie, who was now pressing her hand to Astrid's forehead. By now the other woman were starting to rouse and Ciyrs felt like he was losing control of the situation.

"It's too early," Zadie repeated. "She still has weeks to go before she should be delivering."

Ciyrs relayed the information to Elianna.

"How do they know?" Elianna asked. "She is carrying a hybrid baby."

Ciyrs repeated this to Zadie, who looked at him sharply.

"Do you honestly believe that Ryan left anything up to fate?" she asked angrily. "He knew every detail of everything that he did. We weren't people to him, we were living machines. He followed the development of our babies from the moment that they were conceived and knew with almost perfect accuracy when they would be born. Astrid shouldn't be ready to give birth now."

"I can't stop it," Astrid gasped.

"You'll have to deliver the baby," Elianna said.

"I've never delivered a human baby," Ciyrs said. "I've only been present for one birth, and I didn't manage it. I'm going to need your help."

Zadie looked at the other women.

"You need to stay calm and give us as much room as you can," she commanded. "If you can, get into the seats further up. Astrid needs space."

Ciyrs helped two of the women climb over the seat to sit in front of him and then climbed over into the back section where Astrid lay. She was soaked in sweat now and tears had pooled under her eyes. She gasped again, her back arching with the shock of the contraction, and Zadie reached to guide her back down.

"You need to try to relax," she said. "We can't stop the contractions now. The baby is coming and you have to help it."

"I can't," Astrid said in a tremulous voice. "I can't."

"Yes, you can," Ciyrs told her. "You are ready for this."

Astrid's eyes opened and she looked into his with an insistence that chilled his blood.

"Please," she said.

It was the only word she said, but he knew that it carried with it far more meaning than the single syllable implied. Her fingers had weakly gathered her skirt up her thighs and over her knees, and when he looked down he saw blood spreading across the blanket beneath her. Suddenly her hands fell away from her legs and he saw her eyes roll back in her head.

"What's happening?" Elianna asked. "Ciyrs, what's happening?"

"She's bleeding," he said. "She's not responsive."

"You have to get the baby out," Elianna said. "Now."

The urgency in Elianna's voice jolted Ciyrs into action. He pushed her dress the rest of the way up Astrid's legs and pressed on her belly, allowing Elianna's voice in his mind guide him through urging the baby out of the woman. Zadie cradled Astrid's head in her lap, stroking the sides of her face as she spoke softly to her. Ciyrs worked as quickly as he could and finally a tiny baby emerged into his hands. He gathered him close to his chest and reached for one of the blankets, draping it over the frail, shivering frame. In his arms, the tiny child let out a weak cry just as Ciyrs looked up and saw the dark outline of a planet building on the horizon.

TBC

To be continued...